His Forever
Texas Rose

STELLA BAGWELL

HARLEQUIN
SPECIAL
EDITION

HARLEQUIN®

SPECIAL EDITION™

Recycling programs for this product may not exist in your area.

ISBN-13: 978-1-335-40472-5

His Forever Texas Rose

Harlequin Enterprises ULC
22 Adelaide St. West, 40th Floor
Toronto, Ontario M5H 4E3, Canada
www.Harlequin.com

Printed in U.S.A.

"Do you need to feel loved, Nicci?"

Her heart thudded like a slow, heavy drumbeat. "Sure I do. Don't you?"

Trey looked away from her and made an issue of clearing his throat. The awkward reaction made Nicole wonder if he'd ever talked about the emotion to anyone before now. Had he ever loved a woman? Really loved her with all his heart? If so, it obviously hadn't lasted.

He said, "Sometimes I think about Doc and his family. Roslyn is wild about him. And he feels the same way about her. A guy like me doesn't need that much love. What would I do with it?"

How could she answer his question? She'd never been on the receiving end of that much love either. And if she wanted to be completely honest about it, she'd never given that much of her heart to anyone.

* * *

MEN OF THE WEST: Whether ranchers or lawmen, these heartbreakers can ride, shoot— and drive a woman crazy!

Dear Reader,

Veterinary assistant Trey Lasseter first appeared in *His Texas Runaway*. At that time, I intended for him to be no more than a staff member working in the background at the Hollister Animal Hospital. But sometimes my intentions go awry. In Trey's case, the minute he walked onto the scene, he took on a life of his own and, suddenly, I was smitten with the man.

Not only is he cute and a little goofy, he has the adorable ability to laugh at himself. He's loyal and hardworking, and so humble that he can't imagine a woman loving him just for being him. Over the years, as the Hollisters continued to marry and have babies, I kept thinking that some lovely woman would eventually come along and take notice of Trey. I just wasn't expecting her to be a born-and-raised city girl from Texas!

How could Nicole Nelson, with her stiletto heels and fancy manicure, fall for a rough-around-the-edges cowboy? I hope you enjoy reading how she recognizes in Trey what I saw from the very beginning—that he was the catch of a lifetime.

God bless the trails you ride,

Stella

After writing more than one hundred books for Harlequin, **Stella Bagwell** still finds it exciting to create new stories and bring her characters to life. She loves all things Western and has been married to her own real cowboy for forty-four years. Living on the south Texas coast, she also enjoys being outdoors and helping her husband care for the horses, cats and dog that call their small ranch home. The couple has one son, who teaches high school mathematics and is also an athletic director. Stella loves hearing from readers. They can contact her at stellabagwell@gmail.com.

Books by Stella Bagwell

Harlequin Special Edition

Men of the West

A Ranger for Christmas
His Texas Runaway
Home to Blue Stallion Ranch
The Rancher's Best Gift
Her Man Behind the Badge

The Fortunes of Texas: Rambling Rose

Fortune's Texas Surprise

The Fortunes of Texas: The Lost Fortunes

Guarding His Fortune

Montana Mavericks: The Lonelyhearts Ranch

The Little Maverick Matchmaker

Visit the Author Profile page
at Harlequin.com for more titles.

To my great friends, Pam and Roy Cox,
with love and best wishes, always!

Chapter One

"Doc! There's a problem up at the barn with Frank Whitmore's heifers! The old man is gonna be raising hell!" Trey Lasseter announced as he strode into the veterinarian's office inside Hollister Animal Clinic. "I don't—"

His boots skidded to a stop, along with the rest of his words, as he spotted the attractive young woman standing in front of Chandler Hollister's desk. "Oh—uh, pardon me. I didn't know you were busy with a client. I'll—uh—come back later."

He started backing his way out of the office only to have the veterinarian order him to stop.

"Trey, come back here! Nicci isn't a client. She's

our new receptionist. We were just going over today's schedule before things start hopping."

Receptionist? This woman? She was too refined and delicate to be working in this dusty animal clinic. Was he dreaming, or had Chandler finally cracked beneath his heavy workload?

Trey moved closer as he dared a second glance at the woman. Straight strawberry-blond hair hung all the way to her waist while a pair of silver-gray eyes were staring at him with a mixture of amusement and disbelief. Where in the world had Chandler found *her*? In a high-rise office in Phoenix? She definitely came across as a city girl.

"I was going to introduce you yesterday. But we got called away from the clinic." Chandler gestured toward the woman. "This is Nicole Nelson, but she goes by Nicci. She only arrived in Wickenburg last week, so she's trying to get acclimated to Arizona and working here at the clinic at the same time."

Trey ordered his gaze to remain fixed on her face, but it blatantly disobeyed by slipping up and down the length of her petite figure. A pale pink dress, belted at her tiny waist, stopped just above her knees. Her tanned legs were bare and just as perfectly curved as the rest of her body. It was her choice of footwear, however, that caught the majority of his attention. The nude high heels had extremely pointed toes and straps that crisscrossed atop the foot and fastened around the ankle.

He had to admit the fancy footwear was as sexy as all get-out. But hell, what kind of woman would wear such shoes to work in a small-town animal clinic? The vain kind, or one that lacked good sense?

Trey extended his hand to Nicole Nelson, while worry for his boss was growing in leaps and bounds. This wasn't like Chandler, he thought. No. The man was as practical as the day was long. What had possessed him to hire a woman who looked like she'd never dealt with a sick or wounded animal before. As the receptionist at Hollister Animal Clinic she needed to be prepared to see many.

"My pleasure, ma'am. I'm Trey Lasseter," he introduced himself. "Doc's other right hand."

She arched a skeptical brow at Trey, which promptly caused Chandler to chuckle.

"As much as I hate to admit it, I couldn't run this place without Trey," Chandler told her. "He's a vet technician and has worked with me for more than eleven years now. Most of the time he gives me a headache, but I've learned to live with the pain."

Stepping closer, she placed her small hand in Trey's and bestowed on him a smile that made the Arizona sun appear dim in comparison.

"I'm happy to meet you, Mr. Lasseter. I was just telling Chandler that I hope everyone on the staff will have patience with me while I get the hang of how things are run here in the clinic."

If Trey ever had the chance to touch an angel's

wing, he figured it would feel like Nicole Nelson's hand. All soft and smooth and delicate.

"I'm sure you'll do a fine job," he said, then immediately kicked himself for lying. She'd probably do well to last two weeks here before she went running back to wherever she'd come from. But in this case, telling a fib for the sake of politeness was better than cutting her down with honesty.

"If you're wondering about Nicole's Texas twang, she's from Fort Worth," Chandler spoke up. "She and Roslyn have been close friends for many years."

Oh, so that explained everything, Trey thought. Chandler had hired Nicole because of his wife. Well, at least he could breathe easy knowing that the vet wasn't cracking up.

"That's nice," Trey said inanely. "I mean, that you and Ros will be working together. Doc and I are friends, too. We go way back."

The woman's silver gaze dropped to the front of his shirt where moist green cow manure had splattered a wide swath across his chest and down his left sleeve. The smell was second nature to him, but he figured that was the reason her dainty nostrils were flared in protest. Or maybe it was the fact that he was still holding on to her hand. Either way, he realized it was time for him to move away from the Texas beauty.

Clearing his throat, he dropped her fingers and

inched himself backward until his hip rammed into the edge of Chandler's desk.

A faint smile curved her lips. "I hear the door buzzer," she said. "I need to get back to my desk. Nice meeting you, Mr. Lasseter."

Before he could invite her to call him Trey, she hurried out the door and left him staring after her.

"What were you saying about Frank's heifers?"

"What?"

Chandler's chair squeaked, and Trey glanced around to see the veterinarian reaching for his cowboy hat.

"Frank is going to be raising hell—that's what you said." Chandler levered the brown felt hat onto his head. "What's wrong?"

Trey did his best to push the image of Nicole Nelson from his mind and focus on the problem at hand. "Oh, uh—about a third of the heifers are empty. No calves on the way."

Chandler frowned. "Out of the whole hundred head?"

"That's right. I've written down the tally, but I've not finished the paperwork," Trey told him. "Jimmy is up at the barn right now marking the barren ones."

Chandler whistled under his breath. "You're right. Frank is not going to be happy about this. But he can't rail at us about it. We're just the messenger."

"It's a cinch his bull isn't getting the job done. Think he'll want us to AI the barren heifers."

Chandler said, "Not now. It's February. He won't want babies arriving at the beginning of winter."

"That might be better than no babies at all," Trey pointed out.

"Not if bad weather hits." Chandler shouldered on a worn jean jacket. "Let's go to the barns. I want to look at these heifers myself. We might need to pull blood on them."

Trey snorted. "Frank isn't going to want to pay for that extra expense. He'll accuse you of using him to make an extra dollar."

"He can always get a vet out of Phoenix or Prescott if he doesn't want to use my services."

"Ha! That's not going to happen." He followed Chandler to the door of the office. "Uh, Doc, what's with the Texas lady? Couldn't you find a local to take Violet's place?"

Pausing, Chandler glanced over his shoulder and scowled at Trey. "I probably could've found a local. But Nicole needed a job, and she has plenty of office experience. She's perfectly qualified for the job."

"And she's Roslyn's good friend," Trey dared to add.

Chandler's frown deepened. "That's hardly her fault, Trey. Roslyn has been after Nicole for a long time to move here to Arizona. The job helped make up her mind. If you think that's favoritism, I'm sorry. You'll just have to get over it."

Trey gruffly cleared his throat. "Sorry, Doc. It's

none of my business who you hire to work here. I—well, I'm just a little shocked, that's all. Miss Nelson—uh—she is a *miss*, isn't she?"

Chandler rolled his eyes. "Nicole is single. But knowing you, I'm sure you scoped out her ring finger before she left the room."

"Aw, Doc, I wasn't looking at her *that* close. She just has that unconnected look. You know what I'm talking about."

"Not exactly," Chandler said dryly. "Unless you mean she doesn't look overly stressed and matronly."

Annoyed with himself for bringing up the subject of Nicole Nelson in the first place, he said, "Well, she just hardly seems the type to work in a place like this."

Chandler's brows very nearly disappeared beneath the brim of his hat. "A place like this?"

Trey smirked. "Hell, Doc, cow and horse manure, dust and animal hair, gory wounds and blood—you've been around all that stuff for so long you forget how it might look to someone like her."

"Working at the front office, Nicole won't see too much of that," Chandler replied. "Besides, I believe you're going to find she has a stronger constitution than you think."

She was going to need a whole lot more than a strong constitution to work around here, Trey thought, as he followed his boss to an exit at the back of the building. He seriously doubted the strawberry blonde had the fortitude to stick around this little cowboy town any more than a month, or six weeks tops. But he was going to keep that opinion to himself. Like he'd told Chandler, Nicole Nelson was none of his business.

The sun was incredibly warm for the third week of February, and Nicole had planned to soak up a bit of the sunshine on her lunch break, but just as she was about to carry a sandwich outside, her cell rang.

When she spotted her mother's name on the ID, she released a heavy sigh. Her parents were having a hard time accepting their daughter's decision to move to Arizona, and for the past week and a half, her mother had called at least three times a day.

"Hello, honey. How are you?"

The tone of her mother's voice made it sound as though Nicole had been critically ill instead of moving to Arizona and starting a new job. Biting back a groan, she said, "I'm at work, Mom. I'm on my lunch break."

"I'm aware of the time," Angela Nelson replied. "I purposely waited for your break before I called. Aren't you proud of me for not interrupting?"

Putting her plan to go outside on temporary hold, Nicole sank into one of the gray metal chairs grouped around a long utility table inside the break room. "I need to use these few minutes to eat, Mom. Before I have to go back to my desk."

A short pause came back to her and then a sniff. "Well, pardon me for wanting to make sure my daughter is okay—way out there in the godforsaken desert—miles away from home."

"Is that violin music I hear in the background?" Nicole asked dryly. "If it is, it's not working. I'm well and happy." At least, she would be, she thought, if her parents would allow her to move forward instead of trying to pull her back to a time and place that she wanted to forget.

"All right, Nicci, you've made your point. So, there's no use in me trying to be subtle."

Nicole rolled her eyes at the idea of her mother being subtle. It wasn't possible.

"Your father and I want you to come home," Angela continued. "Where you belong. As of yesterday, he's been promoted—again. And his salary is going through the roof. He wants to help you financially— buy a new home, car, whatever you want."

"That's nice, Mom. Really, it is. But I still have plenty in the trust fund you and Dad set up for me years ago. I don't want or need financial help." Especially from her parents at this stage, she thought ruefully. Two years ago, Mike Nelson had divorced Angela for another woman and left Fort Worth entirely. His adultery had wrecked the whole family. Angela had suffered a mental breakdown, and Nicole had been left to help her mother pick up the shattered pieces of her life. Then a few months ago, Mike had returned, begging Angela for another chance. Ultimately, her mother had forgiven him, and her parents remarried. But Nicole was far from forgetting or forgiving the upheaval the ordeal had caused in her own life. "I'm doing fine on my own. And we've hashed this out a thousand times already. I have no desire to move back to Fort Worth."

"Well, there's always Dallas."

If Nicole hadn't been so frustrated, she would've laughed. "Is there any difference? Other than about thirty miles?"

Her mother released a short, mocking laugh. "We could have a long debate about the differences of the two cities. But your parents would be perfectly happy for you to live in Dallas. At least, you'd be near us. Not way out there—among strangers."

"I'm already making plenty of new friends. And I'm liking it here." She added, "Very much."

"You would say that. Even if you are miserable, you'd be too stubborn to admit it. But anyway, Leah Towbridge—you know, she's good friends with Randy's mother—told me that Randy hasn't gotten over you. That he'll be coming back to Texas soon and wants to connect with you again. That should be enough to get you back here."

Furious that her mother would stoop to using that kind of emotional extortion, Nicole muttered, "I'm sorry, Mom. I have to get off now."

She punched the face of the phone to end the call,

then turned off the sound so she couldn't hear the ringer in case Angela did call back.

Nicole's hands shook as she dropped the phone into a pocket on her skirt and reached for her sandwich. Damn it, she'd moved hundreds of miles to get away from her mother's smothering attention, her father's betrayal and the regretful choices she'd made regarding her ex-boyfriend. She couldn't allow those things to creep in and shadow the new life she wanted to create here in Arizona.

She started to remove the plastic wrap from the sandwich, but tears suddenly blurred her vision, making it impossible to do anything but bend her head and try to sniff them away.

"Miss Nelson, are you okay?"

The unexpected sound of Trey Lasseter's voice caused Nicole to outwardly flinch and hurriedly wipe at her eyes. "Oh! I didn't know you were there."

"Sorry, again," he said. "This must be my day for interruptions."

Nicole swallowed and straightened her shoulders. "Please, you shouldn't apologize. This break room is for everyone. And I—I'm fine—really."

She glanced up to see the man was looking at her with those dark green eyes that she remembered from their earlier meeting. At the moment they were regarding her with gentle concern, which surprised Nicole greatly. He looked like a man who wrestled a steer by the horns just for the fun of it, hardly the type to notice a woman's tears.

"Well, if anybody gives you a bad time up at the front desk, you just let me know. I'll take care of it."

"Oh, it's nothing like that. So far everyone has been very nice and understanding."

He smiled at her as he crossed the room and pulled a small bottle of water from the refrigerator. "That's good to hear. But sometimes folks can get irate and start making threats. Especially if they think they've waited too long, or don't get the appointment they want."

She watched him twist the cap off the bottle and down half the contents before he lowered it away from his mouth. A very nice mouth, too, Nicole thought, as her gaze slid over the set of chiseled lips. The bottom was just plump enough to make for a nice kiss, while the top was a thin, masculine shape that matched his hooded brows.

Clearing her throat, she said, "I've worked in a public job for several years. I'm used to people being rude and impatient."

He gave her a little half smile, which created a pair of charming dimples in both cheeks. The sight had her drawing in a long breath and letting it out. What in the heck was wrong with her? Why was she looking at this man like she was sexually starved, or worse? Was the high altitude of the desert affecting her brain?

"That's good," he said. "I mean—at least it won't be a shock when a rude one does walk through the door."

He was still wearing the same splotched denim shirt he'd been wearing earlier this morning when he'd walked into Chandler's office. The manure appeared to have dried and the process had apparently taken away most of the odor. Now he smelled more like alfalfa hay, dust and sunshine. The triple combination was totally masculine and not at all unpleasant, Nicole decided.

She began to unwrap her sandwich, more to give her hands something to do, not because she was hungry. Her appetite had vanished the moment she'd answered her mother's call. "Have you already eaten your lunch?" she asked.

"No. I usually just eat twice a day. Once before work begins and then when we quit—whenever that might be." He gestured to the bottle in his hand. "Would you like a water? Or soda? Doc keeps the fridge stuffed for the staff. Guess you've already noticed that, though."

"Yes, I noticed. Chandler is not only nice, but he's thoughtful, too." She put down her sandwich and rose from the chair. "I think I'd rather have coffee right now. Would you like to have a cup with me? Or do you have time?"

Nicole didn't know exactly why she was inviting Trey Lasseter to join her. Except that he was a co-

worker and she wanted to have a friendly relationship with everyone on the staff at Hollister Animal
Clinic. Besides, he was nice to look at and easy to
talk to. And anything to divert her thoughts away
from Fort Worth was welcome.

He shoved back the cuff of his Western shirt to
peer at a square silver watch on a brown leather band.
"Sure. That would be nice," he told her. "You just sit
back down. I'll get the coffee. I bet you like cream
and sugar."

Nicole hardly expected him to serve her, but since
he seemed to want to deal with the chore, she wasn't
going to argue. "I do. How did you guess?"

"Oh, most girls seem to like things softer." He
poured two foam cups full of coffee and added sugar
and cream to one of them. As he carried the drinks
over to the table, he said, "I have to be back at the
barns in ten minutes. Jewell Martin is bringing a
load of goats to be vaccinated. She's getting a little
long in the tooth to be doing the job herself. I told
her I could drive out to her place in a couple of days
and take care of the goats there, but she didn't want
to wait. Those goats are her babies."

He handed her the coffee before taking a seat in
a chair kitty-corner to Nicole's.

"Long in the tooth?" she asked with a confused
frown. "You mean she's an older lady?"

He laughed, but then seeing the blank look on her
face, he immediately apologized. "Sorry, Nicole. I

wasn't laughing at you. Jewell is an older lady, but she does have a mouth problem, too. It's the same problem I have with mine. It's always running off when it shouldn't be."

He gave her a full-blown grin, and the expression caused those adorable dimples near his mouth to deepen even more. Nicole found herself staring at him and forgetting all about her sandwich.

"Oh, I see. Because Jewell is older she needs a little extra help from you?"

He nodded. "And sometimes goats can get rowdy as hell—uh, I mean heck. Especially when you're jabbing them with a needle or squirting meds into their mouth."

"Ouch. That sounds awful," she remarked. "But I guess it's necessary to keep them healthy."

"Aw, it's not that bad. About like giving a person a flu shot." He sipped his coffee, then leveled a curious gaze at her. "How are you and Arizona getting along?"

After taking a cautious sip of coffee, she answered, "Good. It's beautiful here, and the weather is especially lovely."

"This time of the year is spring for us. You've come at the right time to get acclimatized. A few more weeks and it'll be as hot as he—heck. But you'll get used to it—after a while."

After a while. Yes, she would get used to her new home. If her parents would respect her independence and understand that she needed a change in her life, Nicole thought ruefully.

"Fort Worth can be sizzling in the summer, plus the humidity. I don't think I'll have any problem adapting to this drier climate. Actually, I'm still working to get everything unpacked," she admitted. "I didn't realize I brought so many things from Texas with me until I took a look at all the boxes stacked around the house."

"The first four years after I graduated high school, I lived in the bunkhouse on the Johnson Ranch. Bunking with a bunch of cowboys doesn't give a guy much room to collect very many things. When I moved closer to Wickenburg, I didn't have much to box up. But that's been years ago, and I've lived in the same house ever since. I'd hate to think of packing all the junk I've collected." He grinned at her. "I'm too sentimental to get rid of things. I still have the first pair of spurs I ever bought. They're cheap ones and falling to pieces now, but I wouldn't part with them. I'll bet you have things like that, too."

She laughed softly, and it dawned on her that Trey had already managed to lift her spirits. Which was surprising. Especially since she'd met him not more than two hours ago. But he seemed warm and friendly. And God only knew how much she needed a kind, encouraging word.

"I do," she told him. "I still have the first doll Santa brought me for Christmas. She's practically bald now, but I couldn't part with her." She eyed him curiously as she sipped her coffee. "You worked on a ranch before you hired on for Chandler?"

He nodded. "The Johnson. I went to work there as soon as I graduated high school. See, my dad is a cowboy, but he moved to Montana when I was just a kid. I didn't want to live up there, so I stayed here with my mom—until she left for New Mexico. That's why I ended up bunking on the Johnson. And that's how I ended up being a veterinary assistant at first and then later I went to college and earned a tech certificate. Mr. Johnson, the owner, said I had a knack for healing animals."

When Nicole had first started dating Randy Dryer, she was drawn to him because he'd had a serious, no-nonsense personality. She'd been looking for a man who didn't view life as a joke, who was disciplined about what he wanted for himself and his future. Roslyn had called him a stuffed shirt, and if Nicole was being honest, she could admit he'd probably been a bit dry at times, even boring. But he'd been safe and trustworthy. If anything, Trey Lasseter appeared to be the exact opposite. A happy, laid-back kind of guy, who smiled his way through whatever life threw at him. And wonder of wonders, he made her want to smile, too.

She said, "That's good—that he helped you find your calling. I get the impression you like your work."

His grin deepened. "I'd be lost without it. What about you? Are you an animal person?" he asked, then chuckled. "I guess that was kind of a stupid question—with you working in an animal hospital, I mean."

His question was pertinent and certainly nothing to blush about, but Nicole felt a sting of color creep over her cheeks. "Your question wasn't stupid. But I feel sort of stupid answering it. You see, I haven't been around animals all that much. My brother—he's older than me—had a dog when we were little kids, and a few of my friends back in Fort Worth had small pets. But I don't know anything about cows and horses and goats or any kind of livestock."

He reached over and gave her forearm a reassuring pat. "Don't worry a bit, Miss Nelson. After you're here awhile, you'll learn more about animals than you probably want to know."

Rising from the chair, he tossed his cup into a trash basket. As Nicole watched him walk to the open doorway of the break room, she realized she was disappointed to see him go.

"There's no need for you to call me Miss Nelson," she told him. "Nicci will do just fine."

Pausing with a hand on the door facing, he glanced back at her. "Okay, Nicci. And you be sure and call me Trey. That's the only name I know how to answer to. Unless Doc gets mad and calls me something worse," he added in a teasing voice.

"Okay, Trey. Thank you for the company."

Her remark appeared to catch him off guard for a moment, and then he winked and pointed to the sandwich lying on the table. "Better eat your lunch. We have a long day ahead of us."

He disappeared out the door, and Nicole thoughtfully picked up the sandwich and began to eat.

We. Strange how Trey's one word made her feel as though she belonged, as though she was a part of something meaningful.

The idea made her smile, and for the remainder of the day, she didn't allow herself to think about her parents, or Randy Dryer or any other miserable thing she'd left behind her. Instead, her thoughts kept returning to the twinkle in Trey's green eyes and the way those mischievous dimples carved his cheeks.

He was a happy guy. And Nicole needed some happiness in her life in the worst kind of way.

Chapter Two

"Ros, just tell me if you don't have time to talk. I realize it's probably getting close to the kids' bedtime," Nicole said as she sat curled up on one end of her couch with the phone pressed to her ear.

"I still have a few minutes before their bath times," Roslyn told her. "What's up?"

With a husband, two babies and a part-time job at Hollister Animal Clinic, Roslyn Hollister was a very busy woman and nothing like the young woman who'd left behind her plush life in Fort Worth more than three years ago. When her friend had first fled to Arizona, Nicole had been more than upset with her—she'd been downright angry. She'd believed Roslyn was crazy for leaving the security of her father's wealthy home. But now Nicole could see that Roslyn had been the sane one all along. The woman had followed her heart and ultimately found love and happiness. If only Nicole could be that brave and make the same wise choices her friend had made, she thought.

"Nothing, really. I'm still trying to find a place for all this stuff I packed in the U-Haul. I must have been crazy. Half of it I could do without. In fact, I think some of it I'm not going to bother unpacking— I'm going to donate it to charity."

Roslyn chuckled. "And I'm sure most of it is high heels, handbags and fashion jewelry."

Nicole laughed along with her friend. "Well, a girl has to accessorize, you know."

"Hmm. Yes, and you do it so well. But think about it, Nicci—where are you going to wear all those things around here?"

"I don't know," she said, then let out a wistful sigh.

Roslyn groaned. "Oh Lord, don't tell me you're already homesick and that you think you've made a mistake by moving out here. I do *not* want to hear it, Nicci! I—"

Grimacing, Nicole interrupted, "Do you think I'm really that wishy-washy and shallow, Ros?"

"Well, not exactly, but you sound—"

"Forget about the way I sound! I'm tired, that's

all. And anyway, what I'm actually calling you about is—Trey Lasseter."

"Trey Lasseter," her friend repeated in a blank voice. "What does he have to do with anything? Uh—unless—did you two have a run-in or something at the clinic? Did he insult you?"

"Oh, great day, no! Quite the opposite," Nicole assured her. "I only met him this morning. And—well—I'm curious about the guy."

There was a long pause before Roslyn asked slyly, "What kind of curious? Like is he a good employee or is he married?"

Nicole let out a soft, knowing chuckle. "Listen, if Chandler keeps someone around as his right-hand assistant for eleven years, I don't have to ask if he's a good employee. I'm just—well, yes, is he married?"

"No. He's never been married. As far as I know, he's never been engaged. Chandler mentioned that he had a steady girlfriend once or twice, but that was years before I moved out here. I think now Trey just has women friends. You know what I mean? He dates, but none of those dates are serious."

Nicole pushed a hand through her hair as she tried to picture him with his arm around a woman's waist and giving her the same charming smile that he'd given Nicole. It wasn't exactly an image she liked. "Oh. Well, I was just curious. He's really cute."

"He's also really not your type."

Nicole's lips pursed into a disapproving line. "How do you know that?"

"Because Trey is country. His life is simple, and that's the way he likes it. You, on the other hand, love bright lights, big city, shopping, traveling—"

Nicole interrupted with an annoyed groan. "There's nothing wrong with a girl enjoying those things. And I hardly see what Trey has to do with any of that."

"Well, if you can't see what kind of problems that might create, then I can hardly point them out to you."

Scowling, Nicole asked, "Why are you bringing up that sort of thing, anyway? None of that was ever an issue between me and Randy. He was a city guy— totally different than Trey."

There was a long pause before Roslyn finally said, "You're certainly right about that. The two men are nothing alike. And the way I remember, there never was much of anything between the two of you— other than boring acceptance. Maybe now that he's finally out of your life, you'll realize you need some sparks. A man that will remind you that you're a woman."

Nicole stifled a gasp. "Ros! Randy was dependable, thoughtful, responsible. I could count on him to—well, not make a mess of my life." The way her father had made a mess of her mother's life, the way he'd ruined any and all chances for Nicole to make a future with Randy.

Oh Lord, she didn't want to think of that now or ever again.

Roslyn's voice broke into her gloomy thoughts. "Randy was boring. And more interested in keeping his muscles bulked up than making you happy. Be glad you didn't follow him to California. You made a great escape."

"That's easy for you to say, Ros. You have a husband who's insanely in love with you and two beautiful kids. You have a wonderful family—your future is all mapped out. Mine is—"

"Yours will take shape if you let it," Roslyn finished for her. "But it won't if you keep looking backward, nursing your regrets. Frankly, Nicci, that would be another huge issue between you and Trey. He's a happy-go-lucky guy. Your negative outlook would turn him off."

Nicole started to argue that point but quickly bit back the retort. She'd not thought she'd turned into a negative person, but she could admit to herself, at least, that the past year and a half had changed her. And not in the best of ways.

She let out a weary sigh. "Am I really that bitter, Ros? Give me an honest answer instead of this syrupy stuff my mom throws at me."

There was another pause before Roslyn said,

"Okay, I wouldn't call you bitter, Nicci. But you're not the fun girl I knew back in Fort Worth. Before—"

"Before the divorce and Mom's breakdown," Nicole finished the sentence. "Before Dad twisted off and ruined our family."

This time her friend was the one who let out a long sigh. "Listen, Nicci, take it from me. Blaming your dad for your misery isn't a good thing. Nor is it right. I learned that the hard way."

Even though her friend couldn't see her, Nicole shook her head. "Your father was an ogre, Ros. He made your life a living hell. You had every right to blame him."

"No. He made my life hell because I allowed him to. When I finally realized I was strong—that I could stand on my own—my life changed for the better. And thankfully it opened his eyes, too. It hasn't been easy, but we finally have a meaningful relationship."

"Yes, everything has worked out for you," Nicole replied. "And I'm glad. But it's different with me. I've made all kinds of silly mistakes. Not to mention my parents divorcing and then remarrying. They act like they're deliriously in love now, but I can't help but hold my breath. I often worry this newfound happiness with them is all an act and that it can't last."

"You have to quit worrying about your parents and think about your own future. You've taken the first step by moving out here and away from them. Now get a backbone and make the most of it."

Nicole leaned her head against the back of the couch and stared blindly at the whirring blades of the ceiling fan. "I called to ask you about Trey and end up getting a lecture on life. But I suppose I needed it. Has anyone mentioned that you've turned into quite the psychologist?"

"That's what having kids does to a woman," she said with a chuckle. "As for Trey, he's an extremely hard worker, a bit of a motormouth and too kind-hearted for his own good."

"Hmm. Well, this afternoon we had a cup of coffee together in the break room. Uh—just for a few minutes. I liked him." Actually, she'd more than liked him. She'd been taken by his rugged looks and warm smile. More than that, he'd had her thinking she could actually be a happy person again. "But you're probably right. We're too opposite to ever be more than friends."

"Nothing wrong with having a friend," Roslyn suggested. "And Trey is the best kind of friend a person can have. If you need help, he's there. If you need cheering or comforting, he's there. He thinks of everyone else before himself. Throughout those dark days after Joel was killed, Trey was a great support to Chandler. He was someone outside of the family that Chandler could talk to about the loss of his father. Their friendship is as strong as an oak. It always will be."

After Roslyn had met and married Chandler, she'd

told Nicole about the tragic death of Joel, the patriarch of the Hollister family. From the way her friend had told the story, the rancher had ridden out to check on a herd of cattle, but later, a pair of ranch hands had found him dead; dangling head first from his horse. Since his boot was still wedged in the stirrup, it had first been believed the incident was an accident. For some reason the horse had spooked and drug Joel to his death. Even the Yavapai County Sheriff had closed the case. But over the long years since, certain clues had come to light that the man could've possibly been murdered.

"Speaking of your late, father-in-law, has progress been made about finding the truth about his death?"

Roslyn said, "Chandler and his brothers believe they're getting close to discovering what really happened. But nothing definitive yet."

"I'll be wishing them luck," Nicole said, knowing how much solving the case would mean to the family. "Now, back to Trey, I was going to say you make him sound like a saint."

Roslyn let out a short laugh. "Not really. Trey has his wild side, too. But you'll have to hear about that from him."

Nicole would have loved to prod her friend further about the man, but a glance at her wristwatch reminded her that she'd already kept Roslyn on the phone longer than she'd intended. "Okay, it's getting late, and I'm sure you need to be getting the kiddos ready for bed. And I need to get busy with more unpacking."

"Billy is quiet for the moment. I'm almost afraid to see what he and Chandler have gotten into," she said with a laugh. "Good night, Nicci. I'll see you at work tomorrow. And I expect your chin to be up and a smile on your face. Got it?"

"I'll do my best. Good night, Ros."

After ending the connection, Nicole placed the phone on the coffee table, but instead of leaving the couch, she scooted to the edge of the cushion and gazed around the spacious living room. It was beginning to take shape, but the remainder of the rooms were still in a bit of chaos with all sorts of boxes and containers sitting around, waiting to be opened and the contents organized.

Nicole had purchased the house sight unseen, but not before Roslyn had sent her tons of pictures and Chandler had checked out the major parts of the structure like the roof, foundation and plumbing. Once Nicole had arrived in Wickenburg, she'd been more than happy with her new residence. The house was old but full of character, with little hidden alcoves and plenty of shelves to hold all her books and whatnots. She especially loved the oak floors, the varnished pine cabinets and open arched doorways. Outside, the street was quiet, and her fenced yard possessed two large shade trees. There was even a large covered porch that stretched across the front of the house and a smaller one to shelter the back entrance.

A year and a half ago, she'd been living in a modern second-floor apartment with a partial view of downtown Fort Worth. At that time, she'd not given much thought to the noise of the traffic or the neighbors on either side of her. Nor to having a yard of her own, or a cat or dog for company. She'd been too busy with her job at the travel agency and dating Randy to think about much else.

But all that had changed when her father, Mike, had confessed to an ongoing affair and his wish for a divorce. Angela turned into a shattered mess, and Nicole had been forced to give up her apartment and move back in with her mother just to help her deal with the daily chores of living.

For the longest, Nicole had believed she was going to be forever trapped with her emotionally crippled mother. She'd had to let Randy move on without her, and during that nightmarish interval, she'd wondered how long she'd have to go on sacrificing and paying for her father's betrayal. To be fair, her older brother, Trace, who lived in Louisiana and worked in offshore drilling, had offered to come help care for their mother, but Nicole had put him off, convincing him that there wasn't any point in both of them disrupting their lives.

Now Nicole needed to follow Roslyn's advice.

She had to quit dwelling on the past and start living for the future.

With that thought in mind, Nicole left the couch and walked through the house to the master bedroom, where boxes of her clothing were waiting to be hung or put away in drawers.

At the foot of the bed, she opened one of the larger boxes and pulled out a red sequined dress she'd worn for a company Valentine party. The compliments she'd received had assured her the dress had been perfect for the occasion. But now the notion of glamming herself up and walking down the streets of Wickenburg seemed ludicrous.

Trey is country. His life is simple.

Nicole and Trey probably were complete opposites, she thought. But hadn't Roslyn ever heard of the old adage that opposites attract?

Smiling to herself, she put the sequined dress back into the box with the other party dresses and carried the whole thing to the closet, where it was going to remain out of sight and out of mind.

Tomorrow Nicole was going to go shopping for a whole new wardrobe, and she would make sure it didn't involve high heels or sequins.

The next evening the last bit of sunlight was slipping behind a ridge of bald desert mountains when Trey knocked on the front door of his grandmother's house. It wasn't often that work took him this far from the clinic and over into Maricopa County, but he'd spent the better part of the afternoon helping a nearby rancher treat a herd of sick cattle. Afterward, he'd decided to take advantage of the close proximity to the one and only relative he had living in the area.

When his grandmother failed to answer his knock, Trey entered the unlocked house and passed through the rooms calling her name. In the kitchen, he found a transistor radio playing on the cabinet counter and a pot of charro beans cooking on the stove, but Virginia Lasseter was nowhere in sight.

When he'd braked to a stop in the driveway, he noticed her car was parked beneath the carport. She had to be close by, he thought, as he stepped onto the back porch. As he peered across the lawn to a small vegetable garden, he spotted her hoeing between rows of leaf lettuce.

"Granny, you have company!"

She looked around and instantly squealed with delight. "Trey! Wait right there! I'm coming!"

She dropped the hoe, then brushed the dirt from her jeans and shirt and trotted over to the porch.

"You don't need to bother tidying yourself up," Trey said with a grin. "I'm dirtier than you are."

Laughing, she climbed the steps and gave him a fierce hug. "I don't care how nasty you are. You look great to your old grandmother."

"Old? Hah! You're only seventy. That's still a young chick."

With another laugh, she pointed to the ponytail hanging over one shoulder. "I found a few more gray hairs yesterday. At the rate I'm going, I'll be silver pretty soon instead of black."

"And you'll still be just as pretty," he said as he smacked a kiss on her cheek. "Need help with the garden?"

"No. Everything is growing. All I need is hot sun and the water hose." Snaking an arm around the back of his waist, she urged him toward the house. "Come on. I'll feed you some beans."

"I didn't stop by to mooch a meal. But I'll accept if you're offering. Are they done?"

"They're done. Been simmering for hours. Are you hungry?"

He opened the door and allowed her to enter the house ahead of him. "For your cooking, Granny, I'm always hungry."

Inside the small kitchen, she didn't waste time pulling out dishes and silverware.

"Want some help setting the table?" he offered.

"No. You go on and wash up. I'll have it ready by the time you get back here."

Five minutes later Trey was sitting across from his grandmother eating the spicy beans with warm flour tortillas on the side.

"What are you doing this far west?" she asked, as she lifted a spoonful of beans toward her mouth. "Working, or did you drive out here just to see me?"

Virginia, or Virgie, as most everyone called her, had been widowed more than fifteen years ago when James, her husband and Trey's grandfather, was killed in a freak tractor accident. Since then, a few of the single men in the area had tried to talk Virgie into marriage, but none had succeeded. She liked her independence.

Chuckling, he said, "You know, I should lie and say I drove out just to see my precious grandmother. But you taught me that lying isn't good, so I won't. I've been helping a rancher, Hoyt Anderson, with some sick cattle today. After we finished with all the doctoring, I decided I was so close to Aguila that I'd drop by to see you before I drove home."

She smiled at him. "I'm glad you did. Doc didn't come with you?"

"No. He had too much to do at the clinic today. He sent me to do this job alone. And it wasn't easy. I didn't bring any of my own horses. I rode one of Hoyt's, and he was a stargazer. I wore myself out just trying to keep him under control."

She nodded knowingly. "I'm acquainted with Hoyt. He comes into Yellow Boot fairly often. I've heard he's a cheapskate."

Virgie worked as a waitress in a café called the Yellow Boot, located less than a mile away in the tiny community of Aguila. Along with needing the income, she loved being around people. Trey was just thankful she was very healthy and didn't have any problem keeping up with the physically demanding job.

"Yeah, he uses baling wire to keep the tailgate from falling off his truck. But he takes good care of his animals, and that's the most important thing."

"Well, he can't take good care of his wife because she up and left him. Guess you knew that, though. Word was that she took off to Reno with some guy who'd just happened to be driving through town. Guess he wasn't as cheap as Hoyt."

"Poor man," Trey muttered.

"Which one?"

Trey laughed at her question, then promptly shook his head. "Granny, you're terrible. We shouldn't be joking about Hoyt's troubles. And anyway, I'm beginning to think no one values marriage anymore. Every time you turn around, someone is getting divorced. Hell, my own parents couldn't even stay together. I'm lucky to be single, Granny. Damned lucky."

Cutting a brown eye in his direction, she leaned back in her chair. "You think so?"

"Damned right," he repeated. "I don't have to worry about a wife running off or cheating or spending every dime I've busted my butt making. Who needs that?"

She tore off a piece of tortilla and ate it before she asked in a sage voice, "Is that how things are with Doc and his wife?"

Trey grimaced before he finally admitted, "Okay. It's not that way with everyone. But Doc and his siblings are a rarity nowadays."

"I see. You're thinking you'd end up in the miserable majority."

"Pretty much."

"Well, when the right woman comes along, you'll see different."

As Trey watched his grandmother's focus return to her food, he couldn't help but think about Nicole.

"Doc hired a new receptionist. Violet had to quit—for family reasons."

She cocked a brow at him, and Trey thought how pretty and youthful she looked in spite of living for seventy years. Her complexion was freckled and wrinkled a bit from too much sun, but the clarity in her eyes suggested she was definitely young at heart.

"Do I know the new girl?" she asked.

"No. She just moved here from Texas. She's an old friend of Roslyn's."

"I see. How's she working out?"

For the past couple of days, Trey had been surprised at how often his thoughts had drifted to Nicole and how much he'd wondered about her. But he wasn't about to admit such silliness to his grandmother. He was way past the age to be daydreaming about a woman. "I guess okay," he answered with a shrug. "I've only talked to her once."

"Does she have a family?"

"If you mean a husband or kids, no. She's fairly young. I'd say no more than twenty-five."

"Oh. That's interesting. What's she like?"

Trey kept his gaze on the bowl of beans in front of him. "She's one of those delicate types. Slender and fine boned with soft skin and long hair that's kind of reddish blond."

"You're telling me what she looks like. I wanted to know what kind of person she is."

"Heck, Granny, she'd have to be trustworthy for Doc to put her on staff. Anything else, I couldn't say. She seems nice enough. And before those little wheels in your head start turning, she's way too nice for me. She wears high heels and smells like some sort of exotic flower."

"What's wrong with that? Women like being women. Even me."

He let out an amused grunt, then reached over and patted the top of her leathery tanned hand. "Yeah, but you're a combination of pretty and tough. If I ever find a woman for myself, that's the kind I need. Especially if I ever get to have my own ranch. She'll need to be rough and strong."

"In other words, you need a ranch hand. Not a soft little thing to hug and kiss and make you feel like a man."

Trey groaned. "Granny, look at Mom and Dad. They couldn't even stay together until I got out of elementary school."

"No. But they're better off apart," Virginia said. "They just didn't fit together, and they both had sense enough to realize it."

Trey gave his grandmother a wry smile. "I guess I should be grateful they fit together long enough to have me."

"That's right." She lifted a pitcher of sweet tea and topped off Trey's glass. "And if you're happy with the way things are now, that's all that matters."

His grandmother had never pushed or nagged him about his private life. If he asked for her advice, she'd give it, then step back and let him make up his own mind about things. It was one of the many reasons he loved her and enjoyed her company.

"If I got any happier than I am right now, I couldn't stand myself," he said, then leveled a pointed look at her. "And speaking of happy, how many marriage proposals have you received so far this week?"

She slanted him a coy look. "Four, I think. But only two of them were serious."

He playfully clicked his tongue. "Only half of them. That's downright terrible. What's wrong with the hold-out guys?"

She snorted. "Nothing. They're just smart enough to know I'm not about to sit around and take care of an old man who's too shiftless to take care of himself."

"And what about the other two? Will you ever say yes to one of them?" he asked.

Her expression turned a bit wistful. "After sleeping with your grandfather for thirty-seven years, it would take a mighty special man to make that happen."

Trey reached over and squeezed her hand. "Guess I can quit worrying about you eloping with one of those old men."

She shot him another coy look. "I didn't say they were all old. One of those marriage proposals came from a fifty-seven-year-old guy. Pretty good-looking, too, if I say so myself."

Trey sat straight up in his chair and stared at her. "Who? Are you kidding me, Granny?"

Clearly amused by his stunned look, she laughed. "No. Why do you look so surprised. You just said I was still a young chick. Apparently, Harley Hutchison thinks so, too."

"Harley! Why, I ought to go beat the snot out of him," he muttered, then on second thought, he arched a questioning brow at her. "Or was he in the nonserious half of that group of proposals?"

"No, Harley was serious." Sighing, she stirred the beans left in her bowl. "I keep telling him he needs a woman young enough to give him children. He says he doesn't want children. He wants me."

Trey was incensed. "The hell he does. What's gotten into him, anyway? I always thought he was a good man."

She scowled at him. "Harley is a good man. And I think you need to stop and listen to yourself."

Trey's mouth fell open. "What does that mean?"

"Just that you're making me sound like I'm a shriveled old prune of a woman that no worthwhile man would take a second look at. Well, for your information, I might not be a raving beauty, but I can still be sexy!"

Her sassy retort caused Trey to put down his spoon and study his grandmother with sudden dawning. "Granny, are you—why, I'm getting the impression that you might have some feelings for Harley. Do you?"

She cleared her throat and reached for her tea. "I guess I do. In a way. He makes me feel young and pretty and worthwhile. But—I believe he's mixed up about wanting to marry me. And anyway, I need to think on it some more before I say yay nor nay."

Trey didn't know what to say or think. Frankly, she'd shocked him. Asking her about the marriage proposals she got every week was something he'd always done out of fun. But this time she'd thrown him a real curve, and he recognized with a bit of guilt that he was jealous of the idea of Harley, a brawny and virile farmer, loving his grandmother. She was the only relative Trey had that lived close to him. And the only one who'd ever really shown him much affection and love. He resented the idea of having to share her company with anyone else.

"I'm sorry, Granny. I didn't mean anything like that. Hell, you could pass for sixty easy. Probably even pass for Harley's age," he told her.

Smiling wanly, she waved a dismissive hand at him and rose to her feet. "You don't have to spread it on, Trey. I'm not angry with you. In fact, as soon as you finish those beans, I'm going to give you a big piece of chocolate sheet cake."

He watched her go over to a row of cabinets she'd painted a sunny yellow color, and as she gathered makings for coffee, he was reminded of exactly how long she'd been living without a husband. He thought, too, of how much fuller her life would be with Harley.

Yours would be a heck of a lot fuller, too, if you'd find a good woman to love.

The voice drifting through his head came out of nowhere, and before Trey could stop it, Nicole's image followed the unnerving words.

Cursing under his breath, he left the table and went to stand next to his grandmother. "You go sit down, Granny. Let me do this. I know where to find everything."

For a moment she looked as though she wanted to argue with him, but then she smiled and patted a hand against his chest. "All right, I'll go sit and you can tell me a bit more about this new receptionist. I might just have to bring one of my dominickers over to the clinic to check on her. The hen, that is," she added slyly.

He rolled his eyes and shook his head. "Granny, you and me both know that there's not a thing wrong with any of your hens or you would've already had them over to see Doc. And I've never known of you to want to spy before. What's come over you?"

With a knowing chuckle she headed back to the table. "Spring is in the air, Trey. It makes a woman start dreaming and a man start thinking."

He'd been doing plenty of that these past couple of days, Trey thought, as he opened a can of coffee and spooned a hefty amount into the brewing machine. And it had all revolved around a strawberry blonde with silver-gray eyes and a smile that could wither the sun.

Chapter Three

By the time Friday arrived, Nicole was getting more into the swing of her job. Nothing was hard about answering the phone, or writing down names, dates and times. The difficult part was trying to figure out which cases to put on Dr. Hollister's priority waiting list and which ones weren't quite so urgent. When it came to their pets, some people were very persnickety. Like Mrs. Daniels, who was standing in front of a long counter that separated Nicole's desk from the customers. The black-and-white Boston terrier was far too large to be holding in her arms, but the middle-aged woman with frizzed blond hair didn't appear to mind the extra weight, or the loud barks directed at her face.

"The only opening I have is at four thirty this evening, Mrs. Daniels. Or you can try your luck as a walk-in, but as you can see, the waiting room is full and you might be sitting for a few hours."

The woman pursed her lips in disapproval. "Nicole, I realize you're new here and don't understand the situation, but I am one of Dr. Hollister's long-running customers. I'm here frequently, and I know if you were to go tell him the dire situation that my darling little Susie is in right now, he'd want to check her out immediately. She won't eat a bite. Not even a scrap of sirloin! This is an emergency!"

Nicole was hardly an expert on dogs, or any kind of animal for that matter, but it seemed to her that the only thing the squirming, barking Susie needed was to be on her own four feet and left alone to do what dogs love to do.

"Uh, Mrs. Daniels, when was the last time Susie ate anything?"

The woman looked properly offended that Nicole had even asked such a question. Dear Lord, where did Chandler find the patience to deal with these types of pet owners?

"Last night, before bedtime," the woman answered. "I gave her a plate of macaroni and cheese and frankfurters. She loves it and I was treating her for her birthday. You see, she turned three yesterday. And don't try to tell me that the table scraps

have upset her tummy. There's something else wrong
with her!"

Nicole was trying to decide the best way to deal
with Susie, and her owner, when another woman
walked up carrying a pet carrier with a yellow
striped cat inside. The animal was emitting a loud,
hoarse meow, which caused Susie's barking to grow
downright ferocious.

Just as Mrs. Daniels turned to give the cat owner
a withering glare, Nicole heard a door behind her
open and close. Glancing over her shoulder, the sight
of Trey entering her workspace left her weak with
relief.

Turning her back to the waiting customers, she
mouthed the word *help* to him. Nodding that he understood, he ambled over to her as though he had all
the time in the world.

Mrs. Daniels instantly directed her ire at him.
"Mr. Lasseter, will you tell this woman that Dr. Hollister is—"

"I'm sorry you've had to wait, Mrs. Daniels, but
it can't be helped. Dr. Hollister had to leave on an
emergency call. He probably won't be back until
much later this afternoon. If you'd like, I can show
you and your dog back to a treatment room and I'll
see if I can figure out what's wrong with her. Then
Dr. Hollister can treat Susie whenever he returns."

Somewhat mollified, the woman sniffed and lifted

her chin to a proud angle before she shot Nicole an I-told-you-so glare. "Thank you, Mr. Lasseter."

"I'll be right with you," he told the woman, then taking Nicole by the arm, he led her away from the counter and out of earshot from the crowd in the waiting room.

"Has Doc really been called away?" she asked, while trying to ignore the way the warmth of his hand was sending tingles up and down her arm.

Trey nodded. "An emergency C-section for a mare on a ranch about twenty miles from here. He'll be tied up for a while. He took Jimmy to help him because I have a little more experience with handling small animals and I'm needed here in the clinic to do whatever I can."

Surprised, she asked, "You mean you're going to stand in for Chandler here in the clinic?"

Grinning, he patted the side of her arm. "Not exactly. No one can stand in for Doc. But don't look so worried. I can handle simple things like fleas or ear mites. Just don't schedule any delicate operations for me to perform," he joked.

"What do I tell the people who are sitting out there waiting and expecting to see the doctor?"

"Most of the clients are accustomed to Doc being called away from the office. The ones that have animals with a serious problem will reschedule their appointments." He winked at her, then added in a teasing voice, "Right now, I'd better see if I can smooth Mrs. Daniels feathers."

She watched him slowly saunter out of the room, while wondering if his laid-back style of dealing with things stemmed from an uncaring attitude or an overabundance of confidence. It had to be the latter, she decided. From what she'd seen so far this week at the clinic, the man worked too hard and cared too much.

In any case, Trey had come along and rescued her when she'd desperately needed help. And once this trying day was over, she was going to make sure he knew how much she appreciated him.

Trey was washing up after treating the last patient, a dog with a flea infestation, when the door to the treatment room opened and Nicole stepped inside.

"Knock, knock," she said, her pretty face peering around the edge of the door. "Is it safe to come in?"

He grinned at her. "Sure. I won't try to stitch up your ear or give you a shot for heartworms."

She stepped into the room. "The waiting room is empty. And everyone left happy—I don't know how you managed it."

He sprayed down the long treatment table with disinfectant and wiped it dry. "One animal at a time. It wasn't that bad. Thankfully, all the problems were simple today and I could deal with them."

She smiled at him. "I guess you've learned a lot from Chandler over the years."

He nodded. "Normally, I just assist Doc with large-animals. That's what I enjoy the most. But in the beginning when Doc first opened the clinic, I had to help him with the small patients, too. Nothing better than watching firsthand. And Doc is a genius. He hates it when I say that, but it's the truth."

"He's a humble man."

She pushed back a strand of hair that had fallen over one breast, and Trey found himself watching the graceful movement of her hand and how the silky hair slipped through her fingers. It was the same color of the mane and tale on his sorrel mare, Lucy. Sort of blond and red with a bit of gold in between. Except that Nicole's hair would be much finer and softer than Lucy's, he thought.

Clearing his throat, he asked, "Did you need me for something?"

A pretty pink color seeped into her cheeks, and like a fool, Trey couldn't help but notice that the blush matched the color of the flowers on her cotton dress.

"Actually, I came back here to thank you. Before you walked up, I wasn't sure who was going to have a meltdown first. Me or Mrs. Daniels."

He chuckled. "Yeah, she can be worse than demanding. It wasn't exactly fair of me to take her ahead of the others, but she can get so overbearing that it's upsetting to the other clients. The way I look at things, it's better to get her taken care of and out of the building than to have an uproar in the waiting room."

"Well, I really appreciate you rescuing me."

"You were doing fine on your own."

She chuckled. "Not if her dog had gotten loose. I expect she would've terrorized the whole waiting area."

"That's happened before. Mrs. Daniels used to have a Doberman and he got loose once. It took about fifteen seconds for the waiting room to empty."

"Oh my," she said with another laugh. "I thought this job was going to be much quieter than the one I had at the travel agency. I arranged and booked travels for corporate groups. It could sometimes get hectic. But this can get a little stressful."

He leveled a meaningful look at her. "Changing your mind about hanging around here?"

Her lips parted at the same time her brows disappeared beneath the bangs covering her forehead. "You mean quit? Leave?"

He nodded and then, with a sheepish shake of his head, said, "Sorry, I shouldn't have thrown a question like that at you."

Frowning slightly, she said, "No need to apologize. Your question didn't offend me, but it did catch me by surprise. I'm curious—do you think I look like a quitter?"

He'd certainly held that opinion of her a few days ago and even voiced those thoughts to Chandler. But nearly a whole work week had gone by since then, and she'd continued to prove Trey's prediction wrong.

"Not exactly a quitter. I was only thinking this job might not be what you expected. Not anyone on staff has it easy around here, including you. In fact, I wouldn't trade places with you for a million bucks. It wouldn't be worth it to have to deal with people like Mrs. Daniels."

She shrugged. "My job at the travel agency could get crazy. Companies planning travel trips for employees were often changing their minds, canceling at the last minute, demanding their money be returned or threatening lawsuits because the trips ended up being less than pleasant. I'm used to demanding people. But here it's different because of the animals. They are what's really important. As for me hanging around—I'm here to stay. I hope that doesn't disappoint you."

Disappoint him? It scared the hell out of him. Even though he'd scarcely crossed paths with her since the day he'd met her, she was constantly in his thoughts. The longer she was here, the bigger the chance of him making a fool of himself over her.

"Not at all." He cleared his throat and glanced away. "I'm glad you plan to stay."

She let out a sigh, and he looked up to see an impish smile curving her lips.

"I'm going to make a confession," she said. "I'm a terrible cook. So if you know a good restaurant in Wickenburg, I'd love to take you out to dinner. That is, if you'd like to go and you don't have anything better planned. It's the least I can do after the way you saved me from Mrs. Daniels."

Trey figured if he caught a glimpse of his image in the mirror right now, he'd be looking at a mighty goofy expression. Aside from working together here at Hollister Animal Clinic, he'd never imagined this woman wanting to spend a minute with him.

"Aw, Nicci, you don't need to do anything for me. That's just a part of the job."

"Listen, Trey, you'd be doing me a favor by joining me for dinner. You can give me advice about which dining spots in town are good or should be avoided."

Join her for dinner? He wondered if, somewhere between the cat with the abscess and the dog with the torn ear, he'd stepped into another dimension.

He tried to chuckle, but it came out sounding like a strangled bullfrog. "You might not like the food that I do," he said.

She laughed, and he decided this Nicole was a totally different woman from the one he'd found a few days ago sniffing back tears in the break room.

"I'm not a picky eater. What do you say? Are you

free tonight? I realize it's Friday night and you might already have a date. If that's the case, just tell me. We can always go at a later time."

He hesitated as his stunned brain tried to assemble a response. If he had any sense at all, he'd thank her for the invitation and tell her he was too busy to go to dinner, or anywhere else with her. Ever. But when it came to women, Doc had always insisted Trey lost his mind.

"Naw. I don't have a date. I—uh, don't have a thing to do except wash a sink full of dishes."

Hell, he might as well have told her his house stayed in a mess. And she probably didn't like messy men. Yet the wide smile that was slowly spreading across her face said otherwise.

"Great. I'll pick you up around seven. How's that?"

She'd pick him up? Lord, he couldn't believe this was happening. "Uh—sounds perfect." He proceeded to give her directions on how to find his place north of town. "If you get on the wrong road or can't find me, just call."

Nodding, she pulled a blank appointment card from a pocket on her skirt and handed it to him. "Better write your cell number on that—I'll enter in my phone later. Just in case I take a wrong turn."

He scribbled down the number and gave it back to her, then on second thought, he asked in a bewildered voice, "Are you sure about this?"

"Sure, I'm sure," she said on her way out the door. "Be ready. I'm always starving."

Trey was still staring in wonder at the empty doorway when Cybil, a tall middle-aged woman with a head full of frizzy blond curls, walked into the room.

"What's wrong?" the vet assistant asked. "I just saw Nicci hurrying back down the hallway, and there's a sheepish look on your face. Did you say something awful to her?"

Only that he'd have dinner with her, he thought wryly.

Turning back to the work counter, he dropped the instruments he'd used to treat the dog into a jar of disinfectant. "Not hardly. Why would I?"

"You wouldn't intentionally. But you open your mouth before you think. And Nicci's a sweet girl. She's not like those girls you dance with at the Fandango."

Cybil was a good friend and a dependable assistant with the small-animal patients, but that didn't mean Trey appreciated her nosiness, especially when it came to his love life, or lack of one.

"I never thought she was," he said flatly.

Cybil shot him a look of warning as she pulled a trash bag from a basket and fastened the top with a tie. "I just think it would be a shame if you ended up breaking her heart."

Trey's short laugh was incredulous. "Me break

Nicci's heart? That's funny, Cybil. You ought to do a comedy act."

Cybil shook her head. "I'm serious. I can tell that Nicci likes you a lot. And I'd hate to see you take advantage of that."

Nicci liked him a lot? Not in the way Cybil was thinking.

"Don't worry. The only thing Nicci will ever be to me is a friend."

Later that evening, Nicole tossed a piece of clothing onto the pile she'd already tried on and dismissed. Darn it, she wanted to look nice, but not overly so. And sexy, but only in a subtle way. A pair of tight jeans might give her the right sort of country flavor, but she had no idea where Trey might want to eat. Jeans might not be dressy enough. On the other hand, he might want fast food, and a fancy dress would look ridiculous.

You're behaving like a silly schoolgirl, Nicole. It's not going to matter what you wear tonight. Trey Lasseter isn't going to look at you in a romantic way. And you should've never been so forward to ask him out in the first place.

Nicole grimaced at her image in the dresser mirror. Maybe she had been a little forward to ask Trey to dinner. But for the past few years everything she'd done had been for someone else, never for herself. It was time she changed.

Seeing that the hands on the clock were fast ticking away, she finally grabbed a mint-green dress with narrow straps over the shoulders, a close-fitting bodice and a straight skirt that belted at the waist. The summer garment was cool and casual, but nice enough, she decided.

Minutes later, she was walking to her car when her cell phone rang, and thinking it could possibly be Trey, she paused to dig the phone from her purse.

The moment she spotted her mother's number on the caller ID, she promptly dropped it back into the side pocket inside her purse and walked on to the car. She wasn't going to deal with her mother's emotional edicts tonight. Instead, she was going to enjoy Trey's company and hope that he enjoyed hers.

Did women prefer striped shirts or plaid? Or would he make a better impression if he wore a solid color, like light blue or gray? Trey considered calling his grandmother for advice on the matter, but then he'd have to explain that he was going out to dinner with the new receptionist, and then she'd really dig into him. Trey wasn't ready for that. No more than he'd been ready to hear Harley wanted to marry Virgie.

Damned man, who did Harley think he was? And why hadn't his grandmother turned him down flat?

Because she's lonely, Trey. Because she might need to feel a man's loving arms around her. Be-

cause she needs something more in life than waiting on diners in a dusty café. Just like you need more than treating a sick cow or horse and coming home to an empty house.

Frowning, he poured aftershave into the palm of his hand and slapped both cheeks in hopes of slapping away the taunting voice going off in his head. He didn't want to hear that kind of nonsense tonight. For the first time in his life, a woman had asked him out. And not just any woman. She was educated and pretty and had real manners. She wasn't the type who swigged down half a beer and then wiped her mouth on the back of her hand. No, Nicole was a lady. A real Texas rose. And he wanted to enjoy tonight. Because he was pretty damned sure it would be the first and last time that he'd get to go out with her.

After slipping on a blue-and-white paisley Western shirt and tucking the tails inside his jeans, he turned out the light in the bathroom and walked to the living room. Earlier this evening, after he'd arrived home from work, he'd hurriedly tried to pick up the worst of the clutter. Even so, dust was everywhere and the floor needed to be swept and mopped, but most nights Trey did well to find time to eat and sleep, much less do housekeeping chores.

He was trying to brush some of the grime from the brim of his brown cowboy hat when he heard a car pull to a stop behind his truck.

As Trey walked outside to greet her, the last of the

day's sunlight was rapidly sliding behind the hills to the west of his house, sending wide swaths of shadows across the porch and the small front yard cordoned off by a fence of cedar post and barbed wire.

She'd nearly reached the yard gate when she gave him a cheery wave. "Hi! I found your place with no problem at all."

"I'd like to say it was my good directions that got you here without a snag, but I'm betting it was your navigating skills."

She laughed. "Oh, if you only knew how easily I get lost. I'm still having trouble remembering the route from my house to Conchita's coffee shop. And that's only a few streets away!"

As she stood beside him at the gate, it was all Trey could do not to gape at her. She was so pretty and soft, and the smile on her face made him feel a whole foot taller than his six feet and three inches.

"That's only because you're new around here. After a bit you'll remember the layout." He gestured to the front of the house. "Would you like to go in? Except for getting my keys and wallet, I'm ready."

"I'd love to go in." She casually wrapped her arm around his, and they walked along the row of stepping-stones that led up to the porch. "But you really don't need to bother about your wallet or keys. I'm going to drive and I'll be paying for dinner, too."

Trey very nearly stumbled. "Uh—that's not the cowboy way," he told her. "We buy a lady's dinner."

She slanted him a cheeky smile. "Well, that's not the Nicci Nelson way. I invited you tonight, so I'll get the bill. You can take care of the next one."

He came close to stumbling a second time. The next one? That had to be a figure of speech, he thought. There wouldn't be a second time. Not with him and her. After tonight she'd have more than her fill of Hayseed Trey.

"Uh—I guess—well, Granny always taught me to never argue with a lady, so I won't."

He glanced over to see her smile had turned soft, and Trey suddenly wondered if it was possible for a man to continue to walk upright after his bones melted. He was still standing and moving one foot in front of the other, but as they climbed the steps and crossed the porch, he didn't feel anywhere close to normal. In fact, he hadn't felt this shaky or breathless since a bull had rammed a horn into his rib cage and punctured a lung.

"Good," she said. "Your grandmother sounds like a woman I'd like to know. Does she live close by?"

"Not really. She lives near Aguila. About twenty-five miles west of here."

He pushed open the door, and after motioning for her to precede him, he followed her inside. "It probably feels hot in here," he said. "Since I knew I'd be leaving, I didn't bother turning on the air conditioner."

She shook her head. "It feels fine. Actually, I'm

learning how quickly it cools out here in Arizona after the sun goes down. In another hour's time I'll probably need a sweater."

Trey hoped not. The dress she was wearing exposed her bare creamy shoulders, toned arms and a hint of cleavage above the V neckline. Covering up all that beauty would be an awful shame, he thought.

"I'll get my things from the bedroom," he told her and gestured toward a couch and two armchairs grouped in a U shape in the middle of the room. "Have a seat."

"Thanks," she told him as she sank gracefully into one of the armchairs. "And take your time. There's no hurry. Unless you have to be up early to work in the morning. I didn't schedule anything early for you and Chandler, but I'm learning that he agrees to jobs on his own and forgets to tell me to put them down on the appointment book."

Trey chuckled. "That's Doc. But no, for the first Saturday in a long while, we're not making a house call, or opening the clinic for a special reason. It's foaling time at Three Rivers Ranch, and Holt needs him."

He fetched the keys and wallet from the bedroom and returned to the living room. The moment she heard his footsteps on the wooden floor, she looked around and smiled at him.

"I was just thinking you have a nice place here. Have you lived here long?"

"About nine years. It's an old house, but it's solid." He made a circular gesture with his hand. "I hope you'll overlook the messiness. I'm not much on house cleaning. And I—well, I hardly ever have company. Unless it's just one of the guys—like Jimmy or somebody like that."

The corners of her mouth tilted upward in an impish smile. "No female guests?"

A hot blush climbed up his neck and over his face. "Me? Shoot, I'll be honest, Nicci, you're the first woman who's ever been here. Uh—I mean, other than Granny. And Roslyn. She and Doc have stopped by together. Back when I had girlfriends—the steady kind, that is—I didn't live here in this house."

Her expression sobered as though she'd suddenly been struck by a sad thought. Either that, or she felt terribly sorry for him.

"I see. Well, I'll be honest with you, Trey. I'm not much on house cleaning, either. This all looks nice and neat. Would you care to show me the rest of the house?"

Something had gone haywire with his lungs, he decided. He couldn't seem to suck in enough air or push it out. Still, he forced himself to walk over to where she was sitting. "I don't mind. But then you're going to see where I piled all the junk that was here in the living room so that you wouldn't see it."

She suddenly laughed, and Trey was relieved to see a smile back on her face.

"You shouldn't have bothered. Not for me. I've only been in Wickenburg a little more than two weeks and I had to start to work right away. So my house is still piled with moving boxes," she assured him.

He reached down and gave her a helping hand up from the chair. "That makes me feel better."

Expecting her to pull her hand away as soon as she was on her feet, he was more than surprised when her fingers tightened around his. Since when had a woman wanted to hold his hand just for the sake of holding it? He tried to remember but couldn't come up with one single time. Unless he went way back to when Lacey still lived in town. But that was several years ago, and he didn't want to think about her or any of the fruitless relationships he'd had in his younger years.

"Lead on," she told him.

With the warmth of her hand wrapped in his, Trey led her through a short hallway and into the kitchen.

"Next to the bedroom, I use this room the most. That's why it's messy," he said sheepishly. "Guess you can see I haven't gotten around to that sink full of dishes yet."

She smiled up at him, and Trey was surprised to see a twinkle in the silver-gray depths. "Don't feel bad. I haven't gotten around to mine, either."

Gesturing toward the cabinets, she said, "These are nice. Did you build them?"

The mere fact that she considered him to be a man with enough skill to do such intricate carpentry work was a huge shot to his ego. Yet at the same time it puzzled him. It was as though the woman looked at him with different eyes from everyone else. And that could only end up causing problems. Because sooner rather than later, she'd see the real Trey. The goof-ball who was good at doctoring animals but inept at most everything else.

"Do I look like I could do carpenter work?"

She stepped back as she swept her gaze over him. "Yes, you do. Can you?"

He gave her a lopsided grin. "I can build a barn and do simple repairs. That's about it. I didn't make these cabinets. They were already together when I got them. But I did tear the old ones out and put these in."

She beamed a smile at him. "See, I was right. You can do carpenter work."

"I wouldn't go so far as to say that," he said.

"Oh, I would. My father can't hammer a nail in straight. And probably wouldn't even if he could."

"What kind of work does he do?"

Turning her back to him, she walked over to the cabinet counter and ran a hand over the marble-like top. "He's an oil and gas consultant."

Trey whistled under his breath. "Guess he makes plenty of money."

"Plenty," she said flatly. "He's not nearly as

wealthy as Roslyn's father, but he's like him in some ways."

"I'm sorry to hear that. Old man DuBose isn't the most likable person. Although he's a heck of a lot nicer than he used to be."

She turned back to him, and Trey noticed there was a wan smile on her face that hinted all wasn't right with her and her father.

"His personality isn't like Mr. DuBose's, thank God, but his drive for money is," she said. "Both men have made tons of it, but neither man has ever been content."

Trey chuckled. "Boy, am I ever safe," he said. "There's no danger in me becoming rich."

She laughed, and he motioned for her to follow him out of the room. "Come on and I'll show you the rest of the house."

She walked over and clasped a hold on his upper arm and the two of them ambled down a short hallway, where he pointed out two spare bedrooms, a bathroom and finally the master bedroom, where he slept.

"Do you have property with this place?" she asked as she stepped inside the room.

For a moment Trey's brain didn't register her question. He was too busy imagining himself lifting her onto the rumpled bedcovers and slowly removing that pretty green dress.

He rubbed a hand over his eyes in an effort to

push the erotic image away. "I'm sorry, what did you say?"

She walked over to the window and peered past the curtain. "I asked if you have any property with the house."

"Oh. Yes. Ten acres. I have three horses. They're necessary for my job—when we do ranch calls. Would you like to look out back?" he asked, while thinking he had to get her out of the bedroom before he said or did something that would make him look like a total idiot.

Nodding, she walked back over to where he stood. "I'd love to."

She latched onto his arm once again, and Trey led her to the kitchen, where they exited the house through a back door.

"The house really needs a porch here, too. But I hate to go to the expense of building one. Especially since I don't always plan to live here. I'm saving my money to buy a ranch," he told her.

She glanced at him with surprise, and Trey figured she was wondering where a guy like him would ever get enough money to buy land, much less the livestock to put on it.

"That sounds like an ambitious plan. Is that something you've always wanted?" she asked as he guided her down the set of wooden steps.

"It is. I'll probably have to work a long time to make the dream come true, but that's okay. The harder a guy has to work for something, the more he appreciates it when he does finally reach his goals. You know what I mean?"

Nodding, she squeezed his arm. "That's one of the reasons I moved here to Arizona. So that I could work for my own home, my own goals."

Did those goals include a man? He wanted to ask her, but he told himself her private plans were none of his business. Like he'd told Cybil, the only thing he could ever be to Nicole was a friend.

Chapter Four

The restaurant Trey suggested for plain, downhome cooking was the Wagon Wheel, an older establishment located in the main part of town. The long, narrow dining room consisted of several small square wooden tables in the front area near the windows and booths lining the back walls.

Authentic wooden wagon wheels holding hurricane lamps hung from the tall ceiling, while the pale green walls were decorated with large photos and paintings depicting the town in its earlier heyday of gold and silver mining. Near the table where Nicole and Trey chose to sit, she noticed a small wall mural depicting a grizzled prospector leading a burro loaded down with packs of supplies.

"This is a neat place, Trey," she said as he helped her into one of the wooden chairs. "Do you come here often?"

"When I'm lucky enough to have the time." He eased into the chair across from her, and after pulling off his hat, he raked a hand through his blond hair. "Usually it's so late when Doc and I finish up the day that I just go home and scrounge up something. Like a fried bologna sandwich."

She laughed. "You can make those?"

"Sure. I have a steady diet of them. Sometimes I change it up and fry salami instead, but it's not as good as bologna."

"Sorry, Trey, you're not going to get bologna in here. But we do have grilled cheese if you're that set on having a sandwich."

Nicole looked up to see that a young waitress with long black hair pulled into a low ponytail had arrived with two glasses of ice water and a pair of menus. Between the smiles she was directing at Trey, she eyed Nicole with open curiosity.

"Hi, Linda. And I don't want a sandwich. I'm going all out tonight. Nicci is buying."

The woman's brows arched skeptically as she settled her gaze on Nicole. "How nice of you to treat Trey. He's solid gold."

Trey's laugh was more like an embarrassed cough. "Yeah, just melt me down and I'd be worth millions," he joked, then gestured to Nicole. "Linda, this is Nicci Nelson, our new receptionist at the clinic."

"Hi there," the waitress said politely. "I'm Linda Barstow. I've been friends with Trey for years and years."

Nicole thrust her hand out to the woman. "I'm happy to meet you, Linda. I'm new in town, and Trey has been telling me this is one of the best places to eat."

The waitress shook her hand. "Nice to meet you, too, Nicole." She looked at Trey and then back to Nicole. "Er—did you two know each other before you came to Wickenburg?"

Nicole answered, "No. I'm from Texas."

"But she's rooting down here," Trey added. "That's what she's planning to do."

"That's nice," the waitress said, then glanced over her shoulder as a bell above the door announced more patrons entering the restaurant. "Well, I'd better take your drink orders. I'm the only waitress working tonight, and it looks like we're going to get busy."

After Trey ordered a beer and Nicole a glass of ice tea, Linda hurried away.

As Nicole began to study the menu, Trey said, "Linda went through hell a few years ago. Her parents were killed in an auto accident down in Phoenix and then she lost her little sister to a blood disease."

Lowering the menu, Nicole looked at him with

dismay. "How awful. Does she have other siblings or family around?"

"No," Trey replied. "She's all that's left of the Barstows. I believe she has distant relatives somewhere in Nevada. But I don't think they get along."

Nicole grimaced. "Relatives can be well-meaning, but they can be smothering, too."

He let out a dry laugh. "That's one thing I don't have to worry about."

Nicole wondered what he meant by the remark, but before she had the chance to ask, Linda arrived with their drinks.

Once the waitress had jotted down their orders and moved on to a nearby table, Nicole turned her attention back to Trey.

"I'm interested to hear more about this ranch you'd like to have," she told him as she pushed a straw into her ice tea. "Have you already chosen a place you want to purchase?"

Nodding, he twisted off the cap on the beer bottle. "Yes. Except that the owner doesn't want to sell. At least, not now. I'm hoping that by the time I'm financially able to offer him a price, he'll change his mind. It's a long shot, but I'm like the little engine that could—I think I can, I think I can," he added with a grin.

She chuckled at his self-description. "This property must be your dream spot."

A wistful look spread over his face. "It is. Part

of the property runs along a tributary of the Has-sayampa River. It's lush and beautiful land. A man could raise some fine cattle there."

"Is the owner using it to raise cattle now?"

He frowned. "No. The man's too old and feeble to do outside work anymore. He mostly just sits on his porch and looks out over the land."

"Aw, that's sad," she said. "I guess holding on to the property brings him a measure of comfort. But that doesn't replace being young and virile and able to do the things he used to do."

"Age is a thief," he agreed, then grinned at her. "But it'll be a long, long time before you have to worry about aging."

"I'm twenty-six." She leveled a curious look at him. "How old are you?"

"Thirty-one. Compared to you, I'm ancient."

"Hmm. You do look ready for a rocking chair," she teased.

He chuckled. "You didn't look close enough. I have two rocking chairs on my front porch."

"One for you and one for a lady friend." Her expression sobered as she thoughtfully studied his rugged face. "I'm very curious about something, Trey. Why don't you have a wife and kids?"

From the incredulous look on his face, it seemed he considered being a husband and father as far-fetched as becoming a brain surgeon.

"Me? With a family? That's—uh—funny, Nicci."

"Why?"

He shrugged. "I'm just not cut out for that kind of life. And the women around here know I'm just a confirmed bachelor. That's why—well, I don't have women knocking on my door."

Intrigued by his response, she said, "Frankly, you look like a family man to me. You don't like women or children?"

His short chuckle was awkward. "I like both—plenty enough. Kids are great. So are women."

"Ah—so, you just don't want one on a permanent basis. Is that it?" She didn't know why she was persisting on the subject. She wasn't interested in husband hunting. Her chance for that went out the window with her mother's nervous breakdown. Besides, she and Trey were completely opposite. They'd never be a match. That's what Roslyn had said. And yet, each time Nicole gazed at Trey's warm smile, she wanted to believe they'd be perfect together.

He coughed and reached for his beer. After a long swig, he let out a long breath and shifted around in his chair.

Seeing that he was terribly uncomfortable, she took pity on him. "I'm sorry, Trey. I'm being nosey. You don't have to answer that if you'd rather not."

A little half grin creased a dimple in one of his cheeks, and Nicole found herself mesmerized by the endearing expression on his face.

"You're not being too nosey. I just don't know

how to answer your question. Except that women like me for a friend. But they don't give me a serious thought."

She found that hard to believe. He was a good-looking man. No, he was more than that, she thought. He was very sexy in a rugged, earthy way. Plus, he was nice and easy to talk to. There had to be women around here who found him attractive. Which made her wonder if he deliberately ignored most of them.

"Maybe that's because all you want is to be their friend," she suggested. "Maybe you're not encouraging any of these women to be more."

He let out another long breath. "You could be right. I've been told that I put out some weird vibes."

Different perhaps, but not weird, she decided.

After a sip of tea, she leaned slightly forward. "What would you do if a woman wanted to get serious with you?"

He laughed, but Nicole could tell it was a nervous reaction more than a sound of humor.

"Probably run like hell. Later on, she'd be glad that I did."

Her gaze met his, and as she studied the green depths, she saw flickering shadows. The kind of darkness that was born of deep disappointments and lost trust. He'd been hurt in the past, she realized, yet he hid it all behind a beguiling smile.

Deciding it was time to change the subject, she

gestured to the mural next to their table. "I've learned that mining played a big part in founding this town."

"Mostly gold. And some silver," he replied. "You might not know it, but there's still quite a few mine claims around here."

Surprised, she asked, "For real? Is any gold actually found?"

"I couldn't say. I've heard of some being unearthed, but I don't think any major veins have been discovered. Thank God for that. I'd really hate to see a modern-day gold rush hit around here."

Nicole said, "Speaking of gold rushes, Roslyn was having a fit for me to move out here a week earlier than I did. The Gold Rush Days festival was going on, and she wanted me to be here to enjoy some of it. Unfortunately, I couldn't get everything packed by then, so I missed the celebration. She says it's a very big deal. Her mother-in-law, Maureen, always throws a big party at Three Rivers Ranch, and the town is always loaded with people and fun things to do."

"Doc always insists that I go to the party at Three Rivers. This last one was a doozy. I think there were at least a hundred people there, and I ate so much I thought I was going to be sick. As for here in town, thousands of people come to the festival every year. Booths and special events are set up on the streets. And there's always the big rodeo and music concerts."

"Did you go to any of the events?" she asked curiously.

"One night of the rodeo. That's about all I could make room for in my schedule. Foaling and calving time is always a busy time for me and Doc." He gestured to the mural of the prospector. "Did you know that Loretta often pans for gold?"

Nicole looked at him with surprise. "You're talking about Loretta at the clinic? The girl who does the bookkeeping and billing?"

"Yeah. She lives up by Congress. It was a big gold-mining town back in the 1880s. Now the area is mostly a ghost town, but there's still a small community of folks around there. Loretta likes to hike the canyons and pan a little."

"That sounds like fun to me. Has she ever found gold?"

"I think she's found a few tiny nuggets. She's stashing them away until she gets enough to make a down payment on a house."

"That doesn't surprise me that she's saving her finds. Loretta seems very down-to-earth and responsible. I wonder if she'd show us how to do it? Or maybe you already know how?"

His thick brows lifted with uncertainty. "Do it? Uh—you mean pan?"

Nicole laughed. "What else would I mean?"

With an awkward chuckle, he shifted around on his seat. "Well, uh—show us how to save money?

She has a degree in business. But yeah, I figure she'd be happy to show you how to pan."

"Us," Nicole corrected. "Me and you. I wouldn't want to go without you."

The look on his face was a mixture of disbelief and bewilderment. "Oh—I don't think, uh—you'd want me along."

"Why not? You're an outdoor guy. Me, I've always been a city girl. But now that I've moved out here, I'd like to learn how to be more of an outdoor girl."

He leveled a thoughtful glance at her. "Guess you don't have much to do around here. Not like what you were used to in Fort Worth with all the fancy shopping places and theaters and things like that."

This wasn't the first time he'd suggested she might be bored by small-town living, and Nicole resented his way of thinking. It was too much like her parents, who continued to insist she'd soon grow bored and want to return to her old home.

Frowning, she tried not to sound annoyed, but frustration wrapped around her words anyway. "From what I understand, Phoenix has all those things, and it's not that far away. But contrary to what you may think, I'm not overwhelmed with the urge to see city lights. I don't have a craving to run to a shopping mall or theater, or concert!"

A look of mild surprise came over his face. "Pardon me, Nicci, I guess I hit a sore spot."

She heaved out a long breath. "I guess you did. A

very sore spot. You sound just like my parents. And I moved a thousand miles away so I wouldn't have to hear them tell me what I needed or wanted to make me happy. I prefer to decide those things for myself."

A wide grin suddenly curved his lips. "I knew there had to be some fire to go with all that red hair. Do you always look so darned pretty when you're— uh, fired up?"

Her mouth fell open, and then she rolled her eyes and chuckled. "I don't know. I've never bothered to look in the mirror when I'm fired up," she admitted, then feeling more than foolish, she reached across the table and placed her hand over his. "Forgive me, Trey. I shouldn't be so touchy. You were just making a reasonable assumption, and I went off like a shrew. I'm not really one of those. It's just that— before I moved out here, things were a little rough back in Texas. I think it's going to take me a while to get past them."

The grin on his face gentled to an expression of understanding, and Nicci felt something inside her go as soft and gooey as melted candy.

"Aw, you don't ever have to apologize to me. I've got a tough hide. You could shoot an arrow right at me and it would just bounce right off."

"Especially if it's a cupid's arrow," Linda remarked as she arrived carrying a tray with plates of steaming food. "If you tried to shoot one of those into him, it would probably break the arrow."

Trey scowled at the waitress while Nicole studied her with amused curiosity.

"You say that like you know him," Nicole said impishly. "I've never seen him without his shirt. Does he wear metal armor under there?"

Linda laughed as she carefully placed the plates on the table. "Well, I confess, I haven't seen him shirtless, either. But I figure there's a bunch of barbed wire under there. To keep all the women at a safe distance."

"Oh, now Linda, you know I use a big stick to keep the females away. Not barbed wire," Trey joked.

Linda looked at Nicole and winked. "Don't believe anything he says. He tells stories. But he's a superman with animals."

Nicole glanced over the table to see that a ruddy color had appeared on his neck and jaws.

"A superman with animals, huh? That's quite a compliment."

Trey laughed. "Talk about telling stories—Linda's really telling one now."

The waitress poured more ice and tea into Nicole's glass and then placed a fresh bottle of beer in front of Trey's plate.

"Remember, Trey, you rushed my sister's cat to the animal clinic, after a stray dog tore a hunk from her side. Doc Chandler sewed her up and it never even left a scar. And she loved you for that."

"Oh yeah, I remember her. She was an orange

tabby," Trey said. "But I'm not surprised that she loved me. Most cats take right up with me."

Groaning, the waitress rolled her eyes toward the ceiling. "Janna loved you, silly! Not Annabelle."

His grin was suddenly replaced with a somber nod. "I loved Janna, too. I'm glad I made her happy by saving her cat."

Linda cleared her throat and took a step back from the table. "Yeah, well, if you two have everything you need, I'll let you get on with your meal."

The waitress walked off, and Nicole thoughtfully watched the young woman until she disappeared through a pair of swinging doors at the back of the room.

Picking up her fork, she looked over at Trey. "You know, I'm very glad you suggested we come to this restaurant tonight. I've learned something important from your friend."

His lips twisted to a wry slant as he sliced into a chicken-fried steak covered with gravy. "That I wear barbed wire and can help care for an injured cat? Nothing important about that."

Smiling faintly, she said, "Those are nice things to know. But I was thinking more about the suffering Linda has endured. It reminds me to focus on the important things. And you know what I've decided? That you and me sitting here enjoying dinner together is one of them."

His fork stopped midway to his mouth as he

looked at her in wonder. "Gosh, Nicci, that's a nice thing to say. It feels pretty important to me, too."

No glib words to try to impress her. No pretending to be anything more than a simple, hardworking guy. Nicole liked his unassuming manner. In fact, she was beginning to like everything about the man. And whether that was foolish or smart, she figured only time would tell.

Normally, Trey was never at a loss for words. But as Nicole drove the two of them back to his place, he couldn't think of a sensible thing to say.

Maybe because his brain was too busy trying to figure out her motive for spending this evening with him. Any idiot could see she didn't need *him* for company. And there sure wasn't any need for her to act as though she liked him. Not really like him in a romantic way.

Where did you get the idea she's thinking of you in that way, Trey? Just because she was nice enough to invite you out? You're a fool if you let yourself start imagining her as a girlfriend. She's just a coworker. Nothing more.

"From the scowl on your face you must be miserable," Nicole said as she turned the car off the main highway and onto the dirt road leading to his house. "I'm sorry, Trey, if the evening has bored you. Hopefully, as time passes, I'll learn more about the clinic and the animals you treat. Then I'll be able to talk shop without sounding too ignorant."

Still frowning, he glanced at her. "I'm not miserable."

She said, "Then you must be feeling ill. You haven't said more than ten words in the past fifteen minutes."

Doc would be splitting his sides laughing at the mere idea that Trey could stay quiet for five minutes, much less fifteen. "Sorry, Nicci. I guess I've been thinking. That's all." He glanced over at her lovely profile illuminated by the lights on the dash panel. "And you don't sound ignorant about anything. You've been great company. Just great."

He could hear her release a long breath, and the sound had him wondering what she could possibly be thinking. That this was the first and last time she'd ever waste an evening on him? No. She couldn't be thinking along those lines, he decided. During dinner, she'd asked him to go panning with her. That didn't sound like she intended to end their friendship—or whatever it was.

"I'm glad," she said. "I didn't invite you out tonight to bore you silly."

Bored? Trey could've told her that he'd never been so wide-awake in his life. Every cell in his body was standing at attention, every nerve was humming like a high-voltage wire.

Instead, he said, "Don't worry. I'm not about to go to sleep."

Less than five minutes later, she was turning into his driveway and parking behind his truck.

Once she switched off the engine, he nervously swiped his palms down the thighs of his jeans. If Candy Anderson, or any of the other girls he often danced with at the Fandango, had been sitting behind the steering wheel instead of Nicole, he wouldn't be at a loss for words. He wouldn't be floundering around wondering what might be the right or wrong thing to say or do.

She turned slightly toward him and smiled. "This has been nice. The meal was delicious."

Her lips reminded him of pink rose petals, and he figured if he ever had the good fortune to kiss them, they would feel just as soft and smooth. "Good. Homestyle cooking is hard to beat," he said, then made a backhanded gesture toward the house. "Would you, uh, like to go in or sit on the porch? I can make coffee."

"Oh, I'm too full for coffee, but I'd love to sit on the porch," she told him.

He'd not expected her to accept his invitation. The fact that she did, and so readily, caused his spirits to soar.

"Great!" He practically jumped out of the car and hurried around to help her out. "I'll show you my rockers."

Laughing, she placed her hand in his and stepped onto the ground. "Okay. But I think I'd better get my jacket first."

He released her hand, and Nicole opened the back door of the car and collected a jean jacket lying on the seat.

"Let me help you with that," he said.

He took the jacket from her and held it open so that she could easily slip her arms into the sleeves. The gentlemanly gesture was unexpected and so was the way her heart fluttered as his hands smoothed the fabric over the back of her shoulders.

"Thanks. I won't shiver now." Not from the chilly air, she thought. But the way her body was reacting to his nearness, she was definitely having to fight off the trembles.

"We wouldn't want that." He gently rested a hand at the small of her back and urged in the direction of the house. "Maybe we should go inside where it's warmer and forget about the porch."

"Oh, I'm not that fragile." She glanced up at him. "But it's nice of you to be so thoughtful."

As they walked through the short gate and down the stepping stones that led to the porch, he said, "I have a feeling you're being extra polite. I'm kind of rusty when it comes to entertaining a woman. And to be honest, I don't know any women like you. I mean,

I'm friends with Roslyn and acquainted with all the Hollister women, but you're different."

"How am I different? Because I'm not from this area?"

"I—that's part of it," he said. "And you're—well, more refined—is what I'm trying to say."

Nicole realized he meant that as a compliment more than anything else, but somehow it didn't feel that way. Rather, it made her feel like he'd lifted her up and set her several feet apart from him. She didn't want to be different from him. She wanted to fit into his life.

She cast him a doleful glance. "Don't put me on a pedestal, Trey. I'm just a regular person. Like you."

"Aw hell, Nicci, no one is like me," he said with an emphatic shake of his head. "Or I should say, no one would want to be like me."

Nicole couldn't stop herself from laughing. "Well, you are a little unique. But that's what makes you special."

They stepped onto the porch, and Trey's arm settled across the back of her shoulders. The weight of it was a warm reminder of just how long it had been since she'd had any sort of physical contact with a man. So long, in fact, that she'd forgotten how it felt to feel a spark of attraction.

A spark? Who are you kidding, Nicole? From the moment this evening with Trey started, you've been experiencing an explosion of thoughts and urges that could only be described as hot and bothersome.

He said, "Come over here and try out one of the rockers. I'll let you sit in Granny's. She's the reason I have two. When she comes for a visit, she likes to sit out here on the porch."

The yard lamp situated on a pole at one corner of the lawn illuminated the wooden rockers. Both chairs were painted hunter green and possessed tall backs. A padded cushion covered in yellow print calico was in one of the seats, and Nicole didn't have to guess that this particular chair was his grandmother's.

He gestured toward the one with the cushion. "You take that one," he said. "It's Granny's."

She sank into the rocker and immediately set it into motion. "I feel ten years older already," she joked. "I hope I don't look it."

He laughed as he took a seat in the nearby chair. "Rockers aren't just for old people. They're good for everybody. The back and forth kind of takes your troubles away and eases your mind."

Maybe she should've gotten her mother a rocker back when her father flew the coop, Nicole thought ruefully. It would've been a heck of a lot better than Angela lying in bed, expecting an anxiety pill to change her life for the better.

She looked over to see he'd stretched his long legs out in front of him and crossed his boots at the ankles. In spite of his tall, muscular frame, he had a litheness about him that made his movements very sensual. Although, she expected he would laugh at that notion. He'd intimated through his conversation that he considered himself a clumsy oaf in lots of ways, and she didn't know why. He actually seemed the opposite.

"Does your grandmother stop by often?" she asked.

"She drives over to see me at least once a month."

"Oh, she drives?"

He chuckled. "An old ton Ford pickup with a floor shift and dually wheels."

"Wow! Exactly how old is your grandmother, anyway?"

"Seventy. But she'd pass for years younger. She's a widow—Granddad died about fifteen years ago. Now she works as a waitress in a little café over in Aguila. That's a community west of here in Maricopa County."

Intrigued, she asked, "She still works?"

He nodded. "She still does *everything*. In fact, I just learned she has a fifty-seven-year-old boyfriend who wants to marry her," he added with a touch of sarcasm.

She glanced at him. "You look and sound sulky. I take it that you don't approve."

He wiped a hand over his face. "Oh, I wouldn't say I disapprove. I just don't want her to lose her head and get hurt."

Nicole couldn't help but chuckle. "If your grandmother has been single for the past fifteen years, she hardly sounds like the type to lose her head."

"Well, no. She's very sensible. I guess that's why I'm a little concerned. Since Granddad died, this is the first time she's ever acted serious about a man. And Harley—he's—I guess most women would see him as a virile, good-looking guy."

"Is that supposed to be a problem?"

The smirk on his face very nearly made Nicole laugh out loud.

"Not exactly."

"Then what's wrong? Is he a deadbeat? A jerk or something along those lines?"

Shaking his head, he looked out over the shadowy yard. "He's hardly a deadbeat. He's a farmer and works hard at it, too. He owns plenty of land and a nice old farmhouse. Lots nicer than the house Granny lives in. And he's not a jerk—I—hell, I guess it just gets to me when I think about my grandmother with a guy like him."

"Not a bit jealous, are you?" she asked, unable to keep a teasing note from her voice.

He slanted a sheepish glance at her. "Okay. I'm guilty. But dang it, for the past fifteen years she's been more like my mother than my grandmother, and she's the only relative I have around here. Guess you think I'm acting like a child."

"No. You're acting like a typical man."

His grunt was full of amusement. "Granny says they're one and the same."

She chuckled and then sat back to study him thoughtfully. "You say your grandmother was more like a mother for the past fifteen years. Did your mother pass away?"

"No. Mom is well and happy. See, my parents divorced when I was a kid. After Dad moved to Montana, Mom stayed here and took care of me. As soon as I graduated high school, she remarried and moved to New Mexico, where a lot of her side of the family still lives. But it wasn't long after Mom left that Grandpa was killed in a tractor accident. So that left just me and Granny. We're the only two Lasseters still around here."

From Trey's happy-go-lucky attitude it was hard to imagine that he'd come from a broken home. She needed to take lessons from him.

"I can understand why you feel a bit overly protective of your grandmother," she told him. "But on the other hand, you ought to be happy for her. I'm sure she gets lonely. And we all need to feel loved."

He darted a hasty glance at her before he turned his gaze on the darkened landscape beyond the house. "Yeah. You're right. And Granny would never quit loving me. No matter what," he murmured.

They both went quiet after that, and just as Nicole had decided it was time she start for home, he turned to look at her.

"Do you need to feel loved, Nicci?"

Her heart thudded like a slow, heavy drumbeat. "Sure, I do. Don't you?"

He looked away from her and made an issue of clearing his throat. The awkward reaction made Nicole wonder if he'd ever talked about the emotion to anyone before now. Had he ever loved a woman? Really loved her with all his heart? If so, it obviously hadn't lasted.

He said, "Sometimes I think about Doc and his family. Roslyn is nuts about him. And he feels the same way about her. But a guy like me doesn't need that much love. What would I do with it?"

How could she answer his question? She'd never been on the receiving end of that much love, either. And if she wanted to be completely honest about it, she'd never given that much of her heart to anyone. Not even Randy. Funny how she was beginning to see that now.

Doing her best to put a teasing note in her voice, she said, "Oh, I don't know. Lock it away in a drawer and take it out whenever you get lonely."

He grunted with amusement, then looked at her and grinned. "Heck, I don't have time to be lonely."

She was wondering how to respond to that when he suddenly rose to his feet.

"I'm a bad host," he said. "Would you like to go in where it's warmer? I can still make coffee?"

Her heart was already hopping around like a

bunny on steroids; the last thing she needed was a dose of caffeine. "Thanks for the offer, but I think I'd better be going."

Leaving the rocker, she closed the short span of distance between them and reached for his hand. His fingers immediately wrapped snugly around hers, and the warmth that emanated from his hand radiated through her whole body.

"This has been such a lovely evening, Trey. Thank you for being nice enough to share your time with me."

The odd expression that swept over his features told her he'd not been expecting such a declaration from her. And she suddenly realized that he was clueless to the effect he was having on her. He had no idea that she was attracted to him, or how much she longed to be close to him.

"It's been my pleasure. Thank you for inviting me."

She continued to stand there gazing up at him, hoping he could read the wanting on her face. When he failed to respond, she let out a long, exasperated breath.

"Am I going to have to bop you over the head?"

His eyes widened. "Have I done something wrong?"

"You haven't done *anything*. That's the problem. I thought you might show your gratitude for dinner by giving me a kiss. Or was it not worth that much to you?"

His features twisted with comical confusion. "A kiss? From me?"

She didn't know whether to laugh or groan. Instead of doing either, she gestured to the darkness around them. "I don't see anyone else around here."

"No. But—uh—have you forgotten who I am?"

"Not hardly. You're Trey. Doc's other right hand. The guy who can sew up a cat better than a neurosurgeon. I think I remember you, all right." She rose up on the tips of her toes and pressed her lips to his lean cheek. "Except that tonight you don't smell like cow manure."

His hand came up to cradle the side of her face, and she closed her eyes as the gentle touch washed over her.

"That's because I spent most of my day with cats and dogs."

Opening her eyes, she found herself staring at his lips. The alluring curve of the bottom one, the fine vertical lines running through both and the chiseled corners guarded by a pair of irresistible dimples.

"The only thing you smell like right now is—a man," she murmured.

His hand slipped into her hair, and with his fingers against her scalp, he tilted her face up to his.

Barely breathing, Nicole waited for his lips to settle over hers. By the time the intimate contact was made, her legs were trembling, and she flattened her hands against his chest in order to support herself.

His kiss was everything she'd imagined and much, much more. Like a double shot of bourbon, the masculine taste of him went straight to her head, numbing her senses to everything but the pleasure he was giving her.

With an unwitting groan, she wound her arms around his neck and opened her lips to his. This time she didn't have to tell him what she wanted; he instinctively knew that she was craving his nearness, that she was hungry for the connection of his mouth upon hers.

Even if a clock had been ticking away the seconds in her ear, she wouldn't have registered how long she continued to kiss him, or how much time had passed since she'd pressed the front of her body against the hard length of his. All she knew was that she felt warm and alive and wanted.

It wasn't until the distant sound of a dog's bark broke through her foggy senses that she realized she'd lost complete control of herself. The reality caused her to quickly step back.

With her gaze glued to the floor, she sucked in a long, ragged breath. "Oh, Trey, I'm sorry! I don't know what happened to me. You must think I'm awful or—worse."

When he didn't immediately respond, she looked up to find a serious expression on his face. The sight of it rattled her almost as much as the kiss they'd just shared.

"Nicci, I—why are you sorry? Because you regret kissing me?"

"No! Nothing like that—" She swallowed hard, and then because she just had to touch him, she stepped forward and rested a hand against the middle of his chest. It was like touching a rock wall, hot from the baking rays of an afternoon sun. And the urge to slip her fingers between the snaps on his shirt and touch his bare skin was so strong it was all she could do to resist.

"I don't regret kissing you. It's just that I've probably given you the idea that I'm—cheap or on the prowl. That's not the way it is, Trey. Not at all."

A little half grin lifted one corner of his mouth. "I could never think such things about you. If you want the truth, I feel darned flattered. In fact, I doubt I'll be able to get my hat on tomorrow. You've just caused my head to grow about two sizes bigger."

His sweetness made tears prick the back of her eyes. "You're so nice to me. Too nice, really," she said huskily. "I hope I haven't scared you off. I hope you'd like for us to spend more time together. Because I'd like it—very much."

His green eyes connected with hers, and in that moment, Nicole decided that everything she'd ever believed about herself, every plan she'd held for her future had suddenly changed.

How could her life shift so drastically in just one short evening? After one sweet kiss?

He suddenly grinned and tugged playfully on a strand of her hair. "Okay. You said you'd like for us to go panning. We'll do that Sunday. Just the two of us—like prospectors in the old, Wild West days. How does that sound to you?"

Like heaven to her ears, she thought, then very nearly laughed at the idea of her hiking a gulch. "I think I'd better go buy myself some sturdy boots."

"And a hat," he added with a wink. "You don't want to burn your pretty face."

Amazed at the joy and excitement she felt at the notion of going out with him again, she laughed.

"Okay, a hat, too," she said, then momentarily pressed her cheek against his. "We'll have fun."

"Sure, we will," he murmured against her hair.

Knowing if she stayed close to him much longer, she'd end up making a fool of herself, she eased away from him and started toward the steps.

"I think I'd better be going. Good night, Trey."

He lifted a hand in farewell. "Good night, Nicci."

She flashed him a smile and then hurried out to her car before she could do an about-face and run straight back to his arms.

Chapter Five

Barring emergencies, the clinic was normally closed on Saturdays, but that rarely meant Trey would get the day off. Chandler used most Saturdays to make remote calls to outlying ranches, so Trey was hardly surprised when he called at five thirty the next morning with two jobs scheduled for the day.

Now it was five in the evening and they were finally driving away from the Flying W to head back to the clinic at Wickenburg.

"I didn't ask you this morning if you had plans for today," Chandler said as he slumped tiredly back in the passenger seat of the truck. "If you did, they're ruined."

Trey chuckled. "Make plans for Saturday? I know you better than to do something like that."

Chandler let out a tired sigh. "I always start out with the intentions of taking the day off, but then the phone rings and I can't refuse."

Trey took his eyes off the highway long enough to glance at his boss and longtime friend. Sometimes he really worried about Chandler's health. Not that the man was ever sick. But he worked himself to the point of exhaustion. Not only at the clinic and with remote calls, but he also handled most of the veterinary work for Three Rivers Ranch, which in itself was a major job.

"Tomorrow is Sunday. You need to rest, Doc. Have breakfast in bed. Let Roslyn spoil you a little."

He let out an amused grunt. "That's not my style. Besides, Evelyn and Billy are always up early. Those two would have my breakfast scattered all over the bed. As for me needing rest, I've figured out how to lighten my workload. It's something I've been thinking about for a long time now."

Trey frowned as he pressed hard on the accelerator and shot past a rattletrap car chugging smoke from the tailpipe.

"How's that? Close the clinic and just work at the ranch?"

"Hell! That won't ever happen. Having the clinic was always my dream." He straightened up in the seat and looked at Trey. "No, the way I figure how to fix this problem is to have another veterinarian working with me. And I don't mean hire some stranger. I want to have someone I've known for years working with me. Someone I can trust. I'm talking about you."

Trey's head whipped around so fast the bones in his neck made a cracking noise. "What? Damn, Doc, I'm no vet. I'm just an assistant."

He swatted a hand through the air. "You're more than an assistant. You've been more than that for years now. All you need is a bit more experience with surgeries and a few more years of college and vet school to get a diploma to certify you're a veterinarian."

"You're helping me get experience by watching you do surgeries. But the diploma is a whole different matter. What are you thinking? That you'll pay some underworld person to make a fake diploma for me? Won't work, Doc. Everybody around here would know it was a forgery."

Chandler groaned. "I ought to knock you in the head."

"You're not the only one who's told me that," Trey said, his mind replaying every word, every touch he'd exchanged with Nicole as they'd stood on his porch last night. He'd never been so stunned in his life when she'd told him she wanted to bop him over the head because he hadn't made a move to kiss her. Him, kissing a woman like her? A part of him still couldn't believe any of those moments had happened, while the other part was finding them impossible to forget.

"I don't do fraudulent things, Trey. And I wouldn't buy you a diploma in veterinary medicine even if I could. I want you to earn it the old-fashioned way. With that nose of yours in a book."

Trey's short cackle was full of disbelief, and then he began to laugh in earnest. "Oh, Doc, sometimes you're hilarious. And the funny thing about it, you're not even trying to be."

Chandler muttered a few curse words under his breath. "What's so funny about you setting goals for yourself?"

Trey grimaced. "I have goals. You know about them. I'm saving up for a ranch of my own. It might take me a while, but I'll get it."

"Who says you can't have the ranch and the diploma? I'll tell you one thing, Trey, you could get a heck of a lot more ranch if you made the money of a veterinarian."

"Well, yeah. But that's a whole lot of schooling, and I'm not smart enough to be a vet."

"The hell you aren't," Chandler shot back at him. "You already have an associate's degree in vet tech. All you need to do is plow forward and get the rest."

Trey smirked. "Sure, Doc. Two more years of undergraduate studies and then four years of veterinary school. In the meantime, I have to make a living. No, you need to find a practicing vet who'd be willing to move here. Or better yet, talk Roslyn into becoming a vet. She's smart and loves animals. And she has a special touch with the small ones."

"Hmm. It's true that Roslyn enjoys working at the clinic, but she loves being a mother to our children, thank God. That's more than enough to keep her busy. Besides, you don't need to be worried about making a living while you're studying. I can take care of that problem."

Trey had no doubt that Chandler could take care of him financially. The Hollister family was one of the richest in Arizona. And for more than a decade now Chandler had added enormously to his wealth from the income of the clinic. Still, Trey had always paid his own way. In fact, as a teenager he'd worked to help his mother put food on the table for both of them. He wasn't about to start taking handouts now.

"You're a good man, Doc. And way too generous— especially where I'm concerned." He shook his head. "Me being a real, certified vet? Your dog is sniffing the wrong trail."

"We'll see," he said, then slanted a sly look in Trey's direction. "I heard you went on a date last night. How did that go?"

Trey eased off the gas as the Hollister Animal Clinic, a large brick building with a spacious parking area, finally appeared on the left-hand side of the highway. "Where did you hear that?"

"Roslyn invited Nicci out to the ranch last night for dinner. Nicci told her she couldn't make it because she was taking you out to dinner." Chandler chuckled. "How did you manage that, ole pal?"

Trey let out an uncomfortable laugh. It wasn't often that Chandler questioned him about his social life. Mostly because Trey didn't have one. Not the romantic kind.

"To tell you the truth, Doc, I'm still trying to figure it out myself. I didn't do anything. Nicci's invitation just kinda came out of the blue. And I couldn't turn her down and hurt her feelings. Seeing how she's new around here and doesn't know a lot of people yet."

"Yeah, I'm sure it was a real pain forcing yourself to go," he said dryly.

"Okay, go ahead and make jokes about it," Trey shot back at him. "But it was nice. Really nice. And we're going out again tomorrow. So there."

Chandler sat straight up in his seat. "Seriously? She agreed to another date with you?"

Trey scowled as he flipped on the blinker and steered the work truck into the clinic parking lot. "She suggested it. And I didn't want to disappoint her," he said, then relented just a bit. "Actually, I'm looking forward to it. We're going panning."

Chandler was clearly floored. "Panning for gold?"

Trey parked the truck near one of the treatment barns and cut the motor. "Yeah, that yellow stuff that makes men crazy," he joked, then added in a more serious tone, "It was her idea, but I think it might be fun. I have a friend who owns some land up near Congress. He's always told me I could pan there anytime I like. I just never took him up on the offer."

Chandler tugged the brim of his hat down on his forehead. "Hmm. On second thought, you might just find yourself a fortune."

"Doc, now I know you've been working too hard. We both know that finding gold, even a tiny nugget of it, would be one chance in a million."

Chuckling, Chandler reached for his medical bag and opened the truck door. "I'm not talking about gold, Trey. There are other kinds of fortunes a man can find."

"Well, there might still be some veins of copper and silver around here, but that's not something you can pick up and put in your pocket." Trey pulled out the truck keys and tossed them to Chandler. "Nicci and I aren't hunting a fortune. We're just going on a little excursion, that's all."

Shaking his head, Chandler climbed to the ground. "I'm not talking about the kind of fortune you put in your pocket."

Trey looked at him with sudden dawning. "Oh, guess you're talking about Roslyn and the kids now."

A clever smile crossed Chandler's tired face. "That's exactly what I'm talking about. And right now, I'm going home to Three Rivers. Good luck on the panning expedition."

"Thanks, Doc. I'll lock everything up here. See you Monday morning."

The veterinarian lifted a hand in farewell and then walked across the parking area to where he'd left his personal truck beneath the shade of a mesquite tree.

Trey was busy unloading the equipment from the bed of the work truck when he looked up to see Chandler driving away. For a moment he thoughtfully watched the vehicle until it disappeared on down the highway.

There are other kinds of fortunes a man can find.

Surely, Chandler hadn't been talking about a man finding himself love, or a family. That would be crazy. Trey had known Nicole only a few short days. Besides, Trey wasn't looking for that kind of fortune. He figured his life was already rich enough. When a man started being greedy, he was deliberately asking for trouble. And Trey didn't need trouble. Not even the kind with strawberry-blond hair and big gray eyes.

Early the next morning, Nicole was hurriedly downing a light breakfast of coffee and toast when her cell phone rang. As soon as she spotted her mother's number on the ID, she cringed with dread and guilt.

For more than two years, she had basically been her mother's caregiver. Now that Angela was well and supposedly happy again, Nicole needed a break. She needed time for herself. Time to deal with the changes her parents' divorce and subsequent remarriage had brought to her life.

Sighing, she punched the accept button and lifted the phone to her ear.

"Good morning, darlin'," Angela spoke cheerfully. "I thought I'd call early before you started getting ready for church."

"I just got home from early Mass. I'm having breakfast now."

"My goodness, you're energetic this morning," she said. "Your father is still asleep, and I'm having my first cup of coffee. You must have big plans for today."

Ignoring the last bite of toast on her plate, she said, "Actually, I'm going out—with a friend."

"Oh, I'll bet you're heading to Phoenix on a shopping trip. I almost wish I were there to go with you."

Oh Lord, spare me that, Nicole prayed. "I'm not going shopping, Mother. Or to Phoenix. We're going out in the countryside."

There was a short pause before Angela's skeptical laugh sounded in her ear. "Really, Nicci, I understand you think you like this new job at an animal hospital, but that doesn't mean you've turned into the farmer's daughter."

Trying to keep from grinding her teeth, Nicole rose from the little breakfast table and carried her plate over to the sink. "I don't just like my job, Mother. I love my job. And why should it surprise you that I might do something outdoors? When Roslyn still lived in Fort Worth, she and I would picnic at the lake. And during the workweek, I often ate my lunch at the park. I'm not afraid of fresh air and sunshine."

"No. But you live in the desert now. It's probably full of rattlesnakes and scorpions and all sorts of things that sting and bite."

"You mean like all those snakes and things in Texas," Nicole attempted to joke.

"Yes, but we're more civilized here in the city," she argued. "I imagine you have to drive miles before you can find a shade tree."

Rolling her eyes, Nicole was thinking how to reply to that absurd comment, when her mother spoke again.

"Are you and Roslyn doing something at the ranch today?"

Knowing her mother was on a fishing expedition, Nicole said, "No. This is Chandler's only day off, and Roslyn always spends it with him and their children. I'm going out with a friend at work. And time is ticking on, Mother. I need to finish getting ready or I'm going to be late. I'll talk to you later."

There was a long, pregnant pause before she finally said, "Well, I get the message—all right, goodbye, Nicci."

The connection went dead, and Nicole didn't

waste time agonizing over her mother's call. She hurried to the bedroom and reached for a pair of jeans and a yellow T-shirt. As she changed into the casual clothing, she thought about all the plans she'd made before she moved to Arizona. None of them had included a man, or giving her heart away. But all of those well-meaning intentions had flown out of her head the moment she'd kissed Trey.

Or had he kissed her? True, she'd initiated the embrace, but he'd definitely followed through and in the most mind-bending way. Since then she'd not been able to get him, or the kiss, out of her thoughts. What did it mean? That she was starved for physical affection, or that she'd finally met the man of her dreams? One way or the other, she was determined to find the answer.

When Nicole arrived at Trey's place, he met her at the yard gate, and she promptly stood on her tiptoes to press a light kiss to his cheek.

"Good morning." She stepped back and gave him a wide smile. "I hope you're feeling like a prospector today."

Beneath the brim of his brown hat, she could see a twinkle in his green eyes. The sight of it made the morning sun behind his shoulder seem even brighter.

"I don't have a burro and pickax," he said with a chuckle. "But I'm ready to try my hand at finding gold—or something."

Worn faded blue jeans encased his narrow hips and long, muscular legs while a khaki Western shirt covered his broad shoulders. He looked so rugged and masculine and so very endearing that she wanted to glue herself to the front of his body and kiss him until they both forgot everything but each other.

The reckless thought warmed her cheeks and made her laugh sound a bit breathless. "I don't have a pickax or burro, either. But I did pick up two pans and a shovel yesterday at the local hardware store. And a few things from the deli for our lunch."

"I hope you know that we'll be lucky if we find one flake of gold, much less a nugget."

His warning was softened with a lopsided grin, and Nicole realized it wouldn't matter to her if they found only worthless rocks.

"No worries. I liken it to fishing. The fun is in the trying. At least, that's what I'm told. I've never really fished," she added jokingly. "But then, I've never panned, either. So this is a learning experience."

"For me, too." He gestured toward his truck. "Let's get everything loaded and be on our way."

It took only a minute or two to move the equipment from her car to his truck. Once they'd finished, Trey said, "I'd better go fetch a jacket. Just in case a cold wind blows in. You might want to come along and visit the restroom before we leave. The trip is long and bumpy."

"Thanks for the warning," she said as she fell into step beside him.

As they walked past the rocking chairs, Nicole decided she probably had been a bit forward for daring him to kiss her. But she didn't regret it.

From the moment she'd met Trey, she'd sensed a gentle innocence about him. Given the fact the man was thirty-one and had probably enjoyed a few girlfriends in his time, the notion seemed laughable. But the innocence she perceived in him had nothing to do with sex. It was something precious and untouched, something that came straight from his heart. And that simplicity was the very thing that drew her to him.

"Come on in," he invited, as he held the door open for her to enter. "Guess you can tell I haven't cleaned anything since you were here the other night. Doc kept me working all day yesterday. But that's not really an excuse. I hate doing housework."

She laughed lightly. "Most people do. Including me. One of these days I might get around to unpacking everything I brought from Fort Worth. I honestly moved too many things out here with me. And I've hardly had time to turn around."

At best, the look he gave her was skeptical. "Why? Are you thinking you might not want to stay here—in Arizona?"

He'd intimated before that she might soon want

to leave and go back to Texas. Did he see her as that flighty and unpredictable? The idea frustrated her.

"Darn it, Trey, do you think I moved over a thousand miles just to turn around and go back?"

He shrugged. "I guess I have been wondering if you might. People do change their minds."

She grimaced. "My parents wish I would change my mind. But believe me, Fort Worth isn't on my radar. It's totally off the map. Now, if you'll excuse me, I won't be long."

Short minutes later, she returned from the bathroom to find him waiting near the door. A faded jean jacket with a ragged collar and cuffs was thrown over one arm. The relaxed expression on his face suggested he'd already forgotten the stilted exchange they'd had moments ago.

"Ready?" he asked.

"All ready," she told him.

Outside, he helped her into his two-seater truck and, after slipping on a pair of aviator sunglasses, steered the vehicle onto the dirt road that led to the main highway.

Once they were traveling northwestward across the desert floor, Nicole could hardly contain her excitement. Not only was she going on an adventurous trek; she was making the trip with Trey.

"Have you noticed my new boots?" She turned slightly around in the seat so that she was facing him.

He glanced down at the scuffed and worn red

cowboy boots on her feet. "If you bought those as new boots, Nicci, someone sure did cheat you."

Laughing, she said, "They're a pair of Roslyn's old boots. We wear the same size, and she kindly dropped them by my house yesterday. She even said I could keep them." Nicole pulled up one leg of her jeans in order for him to see the fancy inlays on the shaft. "Look at this. Thunderbirds on the front and back. Aren't they fabulous?"

After casting another quick glance at the boot, he gave her an indulgent grin. "Just your style."

She tugged her jean leg back in place. "You're laughing at me now."

He shook his head. "No. I'm serious. They're cute and sexy. Just like you."

Liking the definition of his compliment, she flashed him a smile. "I'm sure Roslyn paid a small fortune for them when they were new. I tried to tell her I would just borrow them, but she says they're on their last leg and need new soles. So my plan is to get them resoled and keep them."

"Roslyn is as generous as Doc." He shrugged one shoulder. "Sure, some would argue that the couple has money to burn. But I figure they'd be just as charitable even if they were poor."

"That's true," Nicole agreed. "Roslyn's father has always been rolling in money. When we were just little girls, I remember how he bought her anything and everything. Trouble was, she didn't want three-fourths of the things he bought for her. The majority of the stuff, she gave to me or her other friends."

"Hmm. Why did she give it away? To spite him?"

"Not spite, exactly. She considered her father's lavish gifts as bribes. To make up for not spending time with her and her mother. Ros didn't want to be—well, bought off by her father. You know what I'm trying to say?"

Trey nodded. "I'll never forget when Ros first showed up in Wickenburg. She was very pregnant and so alone. If Doc hadn't helped her, I think she would've just kept on running—to get away from her father. Thank God that's all behind them now. And her old man is actually acting like a decent human being."

Nicole wished she could believe the bad times she'd gone through with her family were behind her once and for all. If her mother backslid emotionally, or her father had another affair, she hated to think what would happen. Most likely, Angela would probably fly straight here to Arizona and expect her daughter to become her 24/7 caretaker all over again.

Pushing that horrifying idea out of her mind, Nicole changed the subject to something pleasanter. "Ros is going to help me learn to ride a horse. Well, actually Maureen and Isabelle will be my teachers. Ros says they're the experts on riding. I'm excited about it. I figure if I'm going to live around cowboys and ranchers, then I need to learn how to ride like a real cowgirl."

"Have you ever ridden before?" he asked.

"Only a few times. Years ago, on a docile, stable pony," she admitted. "But that's not the same as what you guys ride when you're working on ranches."

"No. Our mounts are a bit more spirited." His lips took on a wry slant. "You're not afraid to get on a big horse?"

"Not really. I trust Chandler's mother, Maureen, not to put me on a bucking bronc."

He chuckled. "I'd really like to see your first lesson."

She shot him a playful smirk. "You say that like you think you're going to see a rodeo with me doing the trick riding—accidently."

"I'm teasing," he said. "I think it's good you're going to learn how to ride. Maybe we can go riding together sometime and take our mining pans with us. Doc says there's some old mine diggings not far from his great-great-great-grandparents' first ranch house. Might be interesting to ride over there."

The idea that he was already thinking of going out with her again was enough to send her spirits soaring. "You think the Hollisters wouldn't mind?"

"Gosh, no. Doc's always inviting me to come over and ride anytime I want. There are some really spectacular places to see on Three Rivers. And given the ranch goes for miles and miles, we wouldn't get in anyone's way."

"That would be interesting," she replied. "Did you say great-great-great-grandparents? Three times great?"

He nodded. "From what Doc has told me, Edmond Hollister built the first ranch house back in 1845. He and his wife, Helena, lived there until the big house was built some years later—the one the Hollisters live in now. The original family and their part in settling Yavapai County is in historical records at the library in Prescott if you'd like to read about them."

"I would. I love history." Nicole thoughtfully repeated, "Hmm, 1845. If I'm remembering what little I've learned about Wickenburg's history, the big gold strike there didn't happen until 1863. So that means the Hollisters settled in the area before the rush."

"The Hollister family arrived in Arizona long before the big Vulture Mine was discovered. Doc and his brothers have a theory that Edmond originally came to Yavapai County to look for gold or silver."

"Did he find any?" Nicole asked.

"Doc says, from what they've gathered from old family documents, the man found some of both and used the money to invest in cattle and horses. So that's how the ranch got started."

"That's how it is sometimes," Nicole said thoughtfully. "A person starts out with a certain plan, but halfway there something comes along to change it. Usually for the better."

"Yeah, just like the old saying goes. When one door closes, a better one will open."

She studied his profile. "I believe you've already walked through your better door, Trey. You've found the spot in life where you want to be."

He grunted. "Funny you should say that. Only last evening, Doc implied that I should get more ambitious."

Nicole's jaw dropped. "Ambitious? I can't believe Chandler would say such a thing to you! You work so hard. How could he expect more from you?"

He shook his head. "Doc doesn't think I'm lazy. He says I do the work of two men. I don't think so, but anyway, he—uh—well, this sounds ridiculous, but he wants me to go back to college to add on to my associate degree in veterinary tech and get a veterinary degree. Imagine. Me being a vet? Funny, isn't it? You can go ahead and laugh. It won't bother me."

Nicole had to admit she was surprised by the suggestion, but she hardly found it amusing. "Why would I laugh? You should be flattered he has that much faith in you."

He laughed, but the sound was hollow. "Like I could pass all those chemistry and anatomy classes."

"Why not? You have a brain. All you have to do is make it work. The real question is whether you *want* to be a vet, rather than *can* you become one."

Frowning, he shoved the brim of his hat back off his forehead. "Well sure, why wouldn't I want to be a vet and make big money?"

"The heavy workload, the emergency calls at all hours of the night, the responsibility, not only for the welfare of the animals, but to the owners. And that's just for starters," she answered.

He pulled his hat back onto his forehead. "Doc wants me to be his partner. Which I guess I am in a working sense, just not on the business side of things."

"That's quite an honor."

He looked at her and frowned. "Yes, it is. But I wish he'd never said any of this to me. It's got me feeling mixed-up and guilty. I don't want to let my buddy down."

Nicole could hear a wistful note in Trey's voice. He wanted to dream, even believe that one day he could be a doctor of veterinary medicine. And she wanted to believe it for him.

"Whether you choose to remain Chandler's assistant or become a veterinary partner, he would never think you let him down. I seriously doubt you've ever let anyone down," she said gently.

He cast her a wry glance. "I'm human, Nicci. I've disappointed a few people over the years. We all have—even you."

His honest reply hit her hard, and she turned her gaze out the passenger window. The desert hills they were traveling through were beautiful, but at the moment she wasn't seeing them. She was back in Texas and faced with the choice of letting her mother down, or ending Randy's future plans.

"Yes. I'm guilty, too," she said quietly.

There was a stretch of silence and then he asked, "A man?"

She stifled a sigh. Not for anything did she want him to think she was still pining for a lost love. That part of her life was long over.

"Yes. He's a marine now. I turned down his marriage proposal and he was disappointed. But I made the right choice—for both of us."

Even though she was staring straight ahead, she could feel his gaze traveling over the side of her face. What was he thinking? That she'd callously tossed her boyfriend aside? That she cared only about her own happiness? She could try to explain what had happened with her family and with Randy. She could tell him how her mother had suffered an emotional and physical breakdown after her parents had divorced. Therapy and medication hadn't helped Angela Nelson recover from the loss. The only thing that had seem to help was having Nicole constantly at her side. In the end, when Randy had announced he was leaving for California for military boot camp, Nicole couldn't abandon her sick mother and join him. But spoken words weren't always enough, she thought. Trey needed to discover for himself that she wasn't a self-absorbed person.

"You're saying you'd make the same choice all over again?"

For a long time, she'd regretted letting Randy out of her life. But that was before she'd come to realize that she'd never really loved him. He'd been like a comfortable pair of shoes she'd not wanted to give up. That was hardly the basis for a lasting marriage.

Smiling, she reached for his hand lying on the console between them. "Most definitely."

His hand turned over and wrapped around hers. "I hope I don't ever let you down, Nicci," he said gently, then slanted a grin in her direction. "But what are you going to think if we don't find any gold?"

Laughing softly, she could only think she'd already found her gold in the form of a long, tall cowboy with sparkling green eyes and a smile that made her heart sing.

"That the fun is in the trying."

Chapter Six

Nicole had turned down a marriage proposal. A man back in Texas had loved her enough to want to marry her.

For the remainder of the drive to Congress, Trey tried to push those realities from his head, but the tormenting images of Nicole making love to another man refused to budge from his brain.

He was reacting like fool. Her love life, past or present, was really none of his business. Or was it? Hadn't that kiss they'd shared on the porch made it his business?

It could be your business if you wanted to make it yours, Trey. But you're not a family man. Don't be stupid and let yourself get mushy over Nicole.

Trey was fighting to push the annoying voice out of his head when he spotted the turnoff to his friend's property and steered the truck onto a hard-packed dirt road.

As the vehicle rattled across a pair of cattle guards, Nicole leaned up in the seat and peered out the windshield. "I'm going to make a guess and say this isn't the road to Congress."

"No, it's up the highway," he told her. "This is a friend's land. He raises cattle—that's the reason for the cattle guard."

"Has he ever looked for gold on this land?" she asked.

"He's had several mining companies offer to buy it. But he considers cattle to be his wealth."

"Must be a man who bets on a sure winner," she replied.

"Nothing is a sure winner. All sorts of things can happen to deplete a herd of cattle. The weather, disease, predators, and then there's the market value that can drop on a whimsy."

"I guess there are risks to most everything," she remarked.

Especially when a simple man like himself becomes involved with a beautiful woman, Trey thought. But who said he was involved, anyway? Just because he'd gotten lost in her kiss didn't mean he was about to fall in love with her. No, indeed.

"That ridge of mountains over there looks fairly close. Are we going that far?"

Her question interrupted his thoughts and he followed the direction of her gaze. "No. Those mountains are probably thirty or more miles away. Why do you ask? Are you ready to get out and stretch your legs?"

"I'm fine. And the scenery is gorgeous."

She looked at him and smiled, and Trey wondered for the umpteenth time why she'd invited him to kiss her. Was she one of those women who liked to tease a man? Is that why she turned down the marriage proposal? Because she never intended to have a serious relationship? The idea should give him a measure of relief, but it bothered him to think she might be just playing him along.

Another three miles passed before Trey finally braked the truck to a halt a short distance away from the edge of a gravelly wash.

"This is probably as far as we should take the truck," he told her. "If we walk on up the wash, I believe we'll find a bit of water in this little stream. It would probably make panning easier. Are you up for a hike?"

"Sure," she replied as she peered out at a rocky shelf shading the west side of the wash. "It's so beautiful here. I can't wait to see more."

After he helped her out of the truck, they gathered their equipment and lunch fixings, and Trey loaded everything into a canvas duffel bag that he'd brought along to use as a carryall.

As he shouldered the bag, she said, "That's a lot for you to carry. We could leave our lunch here at the truck and walk back later when we get hungry."

"It's not that heavy," he assured her. "Besides, once we get to where we're going, we might not want to leave for a while."

"Sounds logical. But how will we know when we get to where we're going?" she asked.

Trey laughed. "Good question. Let's just play it by ear. When you start getting good vibes about a place, we'll stop."

"Okay. I'll put out my ESP antenna," she joked.

They took off hiking up the shallow arroyo, and Trey remained close to Nicole's side just in case she tripped over any of the small boulders embedded in the dry creek. Because she was unaccustomed to wearing cowboy boots, he'd not expected her to navigate the rough terrain all that well. But the farther they hiked, the more she impressed him with her sure-footedness.

"Look at all the blooming sage!" she exclaimed as they passed a thick patch of the bushes covered in tiny purple flowers. "It's beautiful. And what are those trees with the yellow and pink blooms? Those are very pretty, too."

"That's salt cedar," he explained. "Most of the

farmers and ranchers here in the southwest call it a monster."

She looked at him with surprise. "Why a monster? It's lovely."

"It's invasive and sucks up an enormous amount of water that's needed for grasses and other useful vegetation," he explained. "And salt cedar trees are very difficult to clear away. But in recent years the pros and cons of the plant are becoming more debated. Because the trees provide a nesting place for birds and that sort of thing."

She paused to gaze at one of the trees. The long feather-like leaves were covered with yellow blooms and a mass of buzzing honeybees.

"Being a city girl and studying business in college, I never learned much about the environment. I didn't realize it was so fascinating until I moved out here and started experiencing it firsthand." She glanced around at him, then promptly asked, "What's wrong? You're looking at me like I'm strange, or something."

He shook his head. "Nothing is wrong. I was just thinking back to when I first met you. Those high heels you were wearing—well, you looked darn pretty, but I was worried."

A knowing smile curved her lips. "Worried? That I might be out of place?"

"A little." Placing a hand on her elbow, he urged

her forward. "Come on. Let's walk on before the bees decide they want us, too."

They walked about a quarter mile on up the creek before a few shallow pools of water began to appear. When they finally reached a spot where a larger pool was partially shaded by willows, Nicole paused and looked around her.

"What do you think about this spot, Trey? Might not be any gold nuggets here, but it's a nice place for a picnic."

"I'm all for it," he agreed.

Trey stashed their lunch in the deepest part of the shade, then carried their equipment over to the water's edge.

Following him, Nicole said, "I almost called Loretta yesterday to ask her for tips on how to do this panning thing. But I didn't want to make us sound dumb."

Laughing, Trey squatted on his heels and shoveled a small amount of gravel into one of the pans. "Why not? We are dumb about it. My guess is that, back in the old days, prospectors must have learned by trial and error. We'll pretend we're back in the 1860s and just starting out."

"Just starting out. I like the sound of that." Flashing him an impish grin, she reached for one of the pans and knelt down beside him. "Maybe we'll have beginners' luck."

* * *

For the next two hours they painstakingly sifted through pan after pan of rocks and gravel. Nicole tried to imitate what little she'd seen about panning on television shows and in movies, but she'd quickly discovered it was much more difficult than it looked to swish out the water and still leave the pieces of rock silt in the pan.

"I can understand why Loretta does this," Nicci spoke as she poked a finger through several colorful rocks. "It's addictive. I keep thinking, the next scoop, and the next pan will turn up a nugget."

"Guess I'm hooked, too," Trey told her. "I keep thinking the same thing."

She looked down the stream to where he was squatted over his pan. The sleeves of his shirt were rolled back on his tanned forearms while the hems of his jeans were wet from wading near the water's edge. For most of the morning, she'd tried to focus her attention on sifting through the endless rocks and pebbles, but even the idea of finding a gold flake or small nugget wasn't enough to keep her gaze from constantly straying over to him.

"Hey, here's something," he said suddenly. "But I think it's pyrite."

Leaving her pan, she walked over and looked down at the small rock he was holding between his thumb and forefinger.

"Oh, it looks like gold! Maybe it is! How can you tell?"

Rising to his full height, he dug a pocketknife from the front pocket of his jeans. "For one thing the color isn't yellow enough. This has a brassy tinge." He sliced the point of the small knife blade over the glittery streak running through the rock. "Not soft enough, either. If this was the real stuff, my knife would leave a mark. It didn't."

He handed the rock to her, and she held it up to the sunlight and angled it one way and then another. "Aw, that's a bummer. But it's pretty. Can I keep it? It might be the closest thing to gold that we find."

"It's all yours," he told her. "But let's not give up. I've heard if there's fool's gold around, there's usually a good chance the real stuff is nearby."

Slipping the rock into her shirt pocket, she turned wide eyes on him. "Wow! If that's true, then we might actually be in the right spot."

"Could be," he said. "But before we do more digging, I think it's time for lunch. What about you?"

"Eat? At a time like this? You've just made a discovery!"

Laughing, he placed his palm on her forehead. "Just what I was afraid of. You've caught gold fever. I should've never brought you out here."

Laughing along with him, she looped her arm around his. "Okay. We'll forget about gold for a while and eat lunch. Actually, now that I think about it, I'm hungry, too."

On a grassy knoll, beneath a shade tree, Trey placed his jacket on the ground to use for a make-shift table. Once they had the food laid out, they sat cross-legged on the ground and munched on fried chicken, potato salad and Western-style beans.

"Mmm. I can't remember anything tasting so delicious," she said. "I must have been hungrier than I thought."

"You've been working hard."

Glancing down at her yellow T-shirt, she hardly recognized it as the same one she'd started out with this morning. The front was blotched with mud and water stains, while her jeans were equally soiled. She could feel that parts of her hair had worked loose from her ponytail and were now glued in sweaty strands against the back of her neck. She didn't need a mirror to tell her she looked a mess. But she didn't care. She'd never felt this good.

"I'm having too much fun to call it work."

"You call digging through shovelfuls of gravel fun?" he joked. "My fingers are about to bleed."

"Really? Let me see." She put down her paper plate and grabbed up his hand. As soon as she turned his palm upward, she realized he was teasing. "What a faker! It would take more than a few rocks to make those calloused fingers bleed."

Their gazes met and locked, and then his hand

gently took control of hers. Nicole's heart began a wild pitter-patter as he drew her fingers toward his face.

"I think I'd better examine yours," he murmured. "Just to make sure they aren't bleeding."

"I—uh—I'm tougher than you think."

She didn't know if he noticed the breathless sound to her voice, but she figured he could probably see the rapid thump of her pulse on her inner wrist and know that he was causing an upheaval inside her.

"Let me see."

To her surprise, he brought the tips of her fingers to his lips and allowed them to linger there just long enough to cause her to lose her breath entirely.

"Wrong," he said gently. "Your fingers are as soft as the wing of a dove."

"Oh." She swallowed, then nervously cleared her throat. "How would you know—about the softness of a dove's wing?"

"I used to have a pair—for pets." His thumb moved slowly over the back of her hand. "Now that I think about it, your skin is softer than a dove's feather."

She was wilting inside, and if he didn't quit touching her hand as though it were a priceless jewel, she was going to fall right into his arms.

"What—er—happened to the—doves?"

"I decided to give them their freedom, and they flew away together. For a while they would show up and eat the feed that I threw out for them. But eventually, they left and never came back."

"Oh, do you think something killed them?"

A wan smile touched his lips. "No. I think they went south, made a nest and had a family. That's the way with nature. The birds didn't need me anymore."

Like a bolt out of the blue, tears suddenly blurred her eyes and forced her to look away from him.

His fingers tightened around hers. "Nicci? Is something wrong? Are you crying?"

He sounded concerned and a bit confused, which made Nicole feel like an idiot for the sentimental tears. He couldn't know that ever since she'd been a very young girl, she'd dreamed of having her own family.

"No! I'm fine." She quickly blinked away the moisture and forced a smile on her face before she brought her gaze back to his. "What you said about the doves and nature. I was just thinking how nice it would be if things were that simple for people."

He rubbed his palm over the back of her hand in a comforting way, and the sweetness of his touch brought an even bigger lump of emotion to her throat.

"To fly away? Or make a nest?" he asked.

Her smile turned wry. "Both, I suppose."

"Life isn't supposed to be that easy for people."

"Guess not." She shook her head and called up the cheeriest voice she could muster. "But that's enough philosophy. I'm ready to enjoy dessert."

He studied her for a moment longer, as though he wanted to make sure she wasn't about to burst into another spate of tears. To her relief, she must've convinced him, because he released her hand and reached for a plastic container holding a few slices of cake.

"Too bad we don't have coffee to go with this," he said.

He carefully maneuvered a piece of the cake onto a paper plate and handed it to her. Nicole quickly took a bite, but she hardly noticed the taste of the chocolate confection. Her mind was too busy trying to figure out why every little thing Trey did or said was affecting her in ways she didn't understand. She had to get a grip on her emotions. Otherwise, he was going to get the idea that she was either crazy, or prone to histrionics.

She said, "If we were real prospectors, we would've been smart enough to bring a pot and make the coffee over an open campfire."

"Hey, that would've been good," he said. "Along with some marshmallows and wieners to roast."

She laughed and was relieved the urge to throw her arms around him and rest her cheek against his chest wasn't quite as strong as it had been a few moments ago.

Once they'd packed away the lunch leftovers, the two of them returned to the spot at the stream where

Trey had found the pyrite. After sifting through several more shovelfuls of gravel, Nicole found another piece of pyrite, followed by an even larger chunk.

With each discovery, her excitement appeared to grow. Trey was relieved to see her mood had lifted, but he still couldn't dismiss the image of her eyes filled with tears.

After she'd told him about turning down the marriage proposal, he couldn't help but think she was living with regrets and those tears in her eyes were for a lost love.

And what if they were, Trey? You're not going to let yourself fall for her. You're smarter than that.

"We're on the right track, Trey. I'm feeling those vibes you were talking about."

The sound of her voice interrupted his nagging thoughts, and Trey glanced over to see her head bent over her pan as she pushed a finger through a clump of tiny pebbles. Even with her damp, dirty clothes and her disheveled hair, she looked vibrant and beautiful. And nothing like the woman he'd met that first day in Chandler's office.

"Not getting tired yet?" he asked.

"Gosh, no!" Her brows pulled together as she glanced at him. "Are you wanting to call it quits for the day?"

He said, "No, I'm fine. I just don't want you to get too tired. We've been at this a few hours now."

She shot him a bright smile. "Not a chance."

"Good girl," he told her, then leaned forward and scooped up another panful of gravel.

He was carefully allowing the water to slosh over the sides when something flashed in the sunlight. Quickly, he dug through the mud and pebbles until he found the bright yellow object. It was smooth with rounded edges, and it had only a single streak of black ore on one side of it.

Excitement rushing through him, he stood up and rolled the pebble between his thumb and forefinger. "Nicci, I think I've found it."

"It?" She echoed the one word in the form of a question before she glanced at him. The moment she saw he was standing, her jaw dropped. "You mean— a piece of real gold?"

"That's what it looks like to me."

She dropped her pan and rushed over to him. Trey held the piece in the middle of his palm for her to see. She drew closer and touched the nugget with the tip of her forefinger.

"Ooh, that's a yellow-gold color, all right! And it feels rather soft." Then she questioned in a half-whispered voice, "Do you think it's actually gold?"

He grinned. "I'd bet the money in my wallet that it is."

She let out a delightful squeal, then flung herself straight at him. "We found it, Trey. The real thing! This is wonderful!"

Laughing, their arms holding each other tightly,

they jumped up and down together with pure jubilation.

When the celebration finally ebbed and they stood catching their breath, Nicole tilted her head back and looked anxiously up at him.

"Oh my, you didn't lose the nugget in all of that, did you?" she asked.

Drawing his left arm from around her waist, he opened his fist to reveal the golden pebble. "No chance."

Smiling, she continued to gaze up at him. "I'm so happy for you, Trey."

"Don't be happy for me," he corrected. "Be happy for *us*. It's ours—together."

Still beaming, she shook her head. "No. That's to go in your savings. For the ranch you want."

Even though the nugget would probably bring no more than two or three hundred dollars, the fact that she wanted him to have it touched Trey deeply. "Now Nicci, that's not how this is going to work. We agreed before we started that we're in this prospecting together."

"Right! So I have a say on how I want to spend my share. I'm investing it in you and your ranch. You can repay me with your first calf crop."

He chuckled, and then, because he couldn't help himself, he pulled her even tighter against him. "Nicci—I—I've never known a woman like you," he murmured.

"I'm glad."

Her words were muffled by the front of his shirt, and he gently lifted her face up to his. "You are?"

"Very glad. That way you won't forget me."

"No chance of that happening, either." His gaze dropped to her lips and suddenly nothing mattered but kissing her, tasting all of that sweetness.

Trey lowered his head toward hers, but the second his lips landed on hers, his brain turned to a mass of swirling fog. With her soft body draped against his and her lips urging him to deepen the kiss, he was totally lost.

Eventually, as the embrace wore on, he began to register the hot sun baking his back and shoulders and a trickle of sweat rolling slowly down the middle of his chest. Behind them, he heard the wind swishing through the salt cedars and desert willows, the faint buzzing of the bees and the distant screech of a hawk. But none of those things were enough to overpower the taste of her lips and the incredible pleasure pouring through him.

At some point, he realized her arms were wrapped tightly around his neck and the front of her body was pressed so tightly to his that her breasts were flattened against his chest. One of his legs had found its way between her thighs, and his hands were gently cupping the fullness of her bottom.

By the time she opened her mouth and invited his tongue to delve deeper, he was only too happy to fulfil her wish. As he explored the ribbed roof and the sharp edges of her teeth, desire exploded in his loins and shot straight to his brain. He wanted her. So much so that he was practically paralyzed with the need to make love to her.

Did she want him as badly as he wanted her? The question was racing through his mind when a loud sound of falling dirt and overturning rocks forced him to pull away from her.

Stunned by the interruption, they both looked to a spot some fifty or sixty feet on down the arroyo to see a small herd of horses descending a steep bank and gathering to drink around one of the deeper pools of water.

"Wild mustangs," Trey said as he struggled to regain his senses.

Swiping strands of tumbled hair from her eyes, she focused her attention on the horses. "I don't think they know we're here," she whispered.

"They know. They're just too thirsty to be concerned about us," he murmured.

The shaggy winter coats of the animals were beginning to shed, exposing darker patches of hair along their necks and around their flanks. Most of them appeared thin from the lack of winter grazing, and their long manes and tails were ratted. Even so, they were a magnificent sight.

She said, "Something about them being wild and free makes them even more beautiful."

"I wish I could adopt the whole herd."

"Why don't you?" she asked.

He turned his gaze back to her face, and when it settled on her pink, swollen lips, desire clenched deep in his gut. If the horses' arrival hadn't interrupted them, how much longer would he have gone on kissing her? How much time would've passed before he carried her off to some grassy spot and made love to her?

"I don't have enough pastureland." He sounded like a robot, but that was only because he couldn't think straight. Not with his body still aching for hers. Not when he was having to fight like crazy to keep from reaching for her.

Turning back to him, she rested her palm against the side of his face. "When you get that ranch you want, you'll have pasture space for plenty of mustangs," she said, her voice full of gentle certainty. "And that's going to be sooner than you think."

Darn, but he wanted to believe her. Not only about the land, but also the passion he'd felt in her kiss. The tenderness in the way she touched him. Did she really want him that much? Believe in him that much? He was afraid to think about it. Afraid these moments with her were all too good to be real.

"You keep this up and I'm going to have a fat ego."

She laughed softly, and then her expression grew somber as her fingers played with the hair curling over his ear. "In case you haven't yet guessed, you're making me feel pretty good about myself, too."

"That's good. I—uh—" Pausing, he tried to assemble the right words to convey how he was feeling about her and the two of them together. But he quickly realized that was impossible. Not without making himself sound like a goofy sap. "Nicci, that kiss—I don't know about you, but it meant something to me."

Her gray eyes were solemn as she studied his face for long, long seconds, and then the corners of her lips tilted upward in an expression so soft it reminded him of a moonbeam, filling his heart with silvery light.

"It meant something to me, too," she whispered.

He wanted to reach for her, to kiss her again and let their desire for each other play out to the finish. He wasn't sure when, or if, there would be a right time for them to make love. But something told him that now definitely wasn't the time to put their relationship to the test.

Smiling down at her, he clasped a hand around her arm and turned her back to the stream. "Come on. We still have a few hours of sunlight left. It's time we got back to being prospectors."

Laughing, she squeezed his hand. "One nugget found and several more to follow."

Off to their left, the herd of mustangs finished drinking, then disappeared on down the arroyo. As

Trey watched them go, Nicole's prediction about him getting a ranch of his own circled through his thoughts once again.

The land, the cattle and the horses would mean nothing to him without her at his side. Even if she hadn't realized that fact yet, he had. And it was a damned scary feeling.

Chapter Seven

"Trey, take the end of this tape measure and start walking. Don't stop until I tell you to."

Trey turned a frown on Chandler. The two men were at the large barn that sat on a high knoll behind the animal clinic. Five minutes ago, they had finished doctoring a small herd of cattle suffering pink eye and were about to leave for a ranch call up in the northern part of Yavapai County. A job that, if they were lucky, would get them back here to the clinic by closing time.

"What are you doing? I thought we were driving up to the Bar 40 to take care of those bulls for Mr. Seeley."

"We are," Chandler told him. "This won't take

five minutes." He thrust the end of the metal tape at Trey. "Get going. Straight north from where we're standing."

Trey took off walking with the tape unfurling behind him. When Chandler finally called out for him to stop, Trey turned and looked back at his boss for further instructions.

"That's eighty feet. Think that will give us enough space?" Chandler asked.

Trey glanced around at his surroundings. Off to the left were several holding pens made of iron pipe, beyond was a loafing shed and next to it was a larger barn they used for examining cattle.

"Depends on what the space is for," Trey answered. "More parking area for trucks and trailers?"

Rolling in the metal tape, Chandler started walking toward the spot where Trey was standing. "Heck no! We already have plenty of room for parking. Where is your mind anyway? Don't you remember me talking about a new stalling barn for the horses?"

Trey could've told him that his mind was stuck on the clinic's receptionist. But he wasn't ready to admit to Chandler that he was already a cooked goose. Or that Nicole had him so mixed-up he hardly knew whether he was coming or going.

Biting back a sigh, he said, "I remember. But that's been months ago. I thought you'd scrapped the idea for a bigger and better horse facility."

"Why would I scrap it? The hospital needs improvements, and I've finally located a contractor to do the work."

"I hope he's better than the last one who put a new roof on the clinic."

Chandler groaned as he slipped the small tape measure into the pocket of his jeans. "Don't remind me of that disaster. No, this guy does excellent work, and he's dependable. All I need to do is make sure I have the blueprint designs exactly how I want everything."

Trey shot him a wry look. "You don't want a stalling barn. You want a horse hotel with all the amenities. Like air-conditioning, heating and a therapy pool."

"What's wrong with that? A sick or injured horse deserves the best of care. Extra comfort means faster recovery. Plus, the more available treatments I have, the better. I've talked Blake into building one just like it on the ranch. Holt has needed such a facility for a long time. And it will make things much easier for me in both places."

"You already have a damned nice foaling barn on Three Rivers. It has luxury stalls."

"That's for the brood mares and foals. Holt needs this for the whole remuda—'cause there's hardly a day goes by that a few of them don't require treatment for one thing or another."

Trey shook his head. "You're talking about lots

of money, Doc. You think it will actually pay off in the end?"

"I'm not worried about the profit," he said. "Not here at the clinic or on the ranch."

No, Trey thought, Chandler was all about the care of the animal. Not the cost.

The two men left the knoll and began walking toward the white work truck they intended to drive to the Bar 40.

"Speaking of money," Chandler said, "I heard you found a small fortune on your panning expedition this past Sunday. Why hadn't you mentioned it to me?"

Two days had passed since Trey and Nicole had panned the arroyo up near Congress, but the time they'd spent together was still just as vivid in Trey's mind as if it had just happened. Before the waning sunlight had finally forced them to leave the stream, he and Nicole ended up finding three more gold nuggets. But compared to the passionate kiss they'd shared, the gold was insignificant to Trey. Now the memory of having her in his arms was burning a hole right through his brain.

Not bothering to look in Chandler's direction, he said, "I guess you heard that from Ros."

"I hate to say it, but she's almost like a mother hen to Nicci. I've told Ros she needs to mind her own business, but they've been friends since they were little girls."

"No matter. It's no secret," Trey said, while wondering what Chandler really thought about Nicci spending time with his assistant.

"How much gold did you find?" Chandler asked.

"I'd say maybe five or six hundred dollars' worth. Give or take a little. When I get a chance, I'll take the stuff to an assay office and find out the actual value of it."

By now the two men had reached the truck. After they both climbed inside and buckled their seat belts, Chandler looked over at him.

"Didn't Nicci find any gold?"

Trey started the engine. "Two pieces. But she gave it to me. For my ranch savings." He reversed the truck, then turned it onto the highway. "Doc, would you call Nicci a wealthy woman?"

Chandler thoughtfully rubbed his chin. "I couldn't say for sure. I've heard Ros say that Nicci's parents have plenty of money, but whether they share their wealth with Nicci is another matter. Or whether Nicci would accept it, would be hard to say. She doesn't live like she has an abundance of money. And she does need to work to support herself. Why do you ask?"

Feeling a bit foolish, he shrugged. "I just wondered, that's all."

As the truck picked up speed, Chandler settled comfortably back in the seat. "I think what you're really wondering is how long she's going to continue to make her home around here. Right?"

Trey cast him a sheepish look. "Well, it's a reasonable question. She's different from us. And she still has strings attached to Fort Worth. Sometimes I get the feeling those strings are always tugging on her."

Chandler frowned. "She's trying to break them. Especially the strings her mother has thrown around her. Although, to Nicci, they probably feel more like chains than strings."

"What do you mean? What's the problem with her mother? She one of those smothering sorts?"

Chandler shook his head. "She needs to tell you all about that. Not me. Besides, I only know bits of the situation—and that's only because Ros has told me."

Other than mentioning the marriage proposal, Nicci had not shared all that much about her life back in Texas, and Trey was reluctant to push her for information. Especially when she wasn't pressing him for details about his own past.

"She's told me that before she moved out here, she worked for a travel agency, that she studied business in college and that she had a boyfriend who wanted to marry her but she turned him down."

He could feel Chandler eyeing him with curiosity. "What have you told her about yourself?"

Trey's chuckle was a mocking sound. "Now Doc, you know I'm an open book. Besides, me and Nicci are just friends. That's all a guy like me can be to a woman like her. I don't want to have a serious girl-friend. Dating a woman now and then is enough for me."

Rolling his eyes in Trey's direction, Chandler quipped, "Is that so?"

Trey glowered back at him. "Heck yes, it's so! And you know it. Don't try to act like you've for-gotten the messes I got into ten years ago when I tried to be more than friends with a woman. First with Rhonda and then with Lacey." Pressing harder on the accelerator, he fixed his eyes on the broken white line separating the two lanes of traffic. "You would think I learned my lesson with Rhonda when I got the idea that she actually wanted to be my wife. But after she left for greener pastures, I licked my wounds and tried my luck with Lacey. When she walked away, that was enough for me."

Chandler's only response to that was a tired grunt.

Trey frowned at him. "I know what you're think-ing. That I shouldn't blame either one of them. Well, you're right. Both of those women could see I was never going to be anything special. That I could never give a wife the things she needed or wanted."

Chandler let out a caustic laugh. "Oh sure. Even a one-eyed woman could see you couldn't give her a sixty-foot yacht, and a three-story house with a kidney-shaped swimming pool, or a four-car ga-rage filled with a pair of Maseratis and a couple of Corvette convertibles. She'd probably be expecting you to have enough money in the bank to travel the world, too. No. I don't expect you could give a woman those things. So it's best that Rhonda and Lacey saw you for the loser you are and moved on."

Trey snorted. "All right, poke fun at me. I don't care. At least I know my limitations."

Chandler scowled at him. "Damn it, Trey, that's your problem, right there! You look at your limitations instead of the blessings you've been given and the assets you have. But you know what? I think for the first time in your life a woman has come along who sees the real Trey Lasseter and what he stands for."

"You mean Nicci? Well yes, I expect she does. That's why we're just friends. I make her smile and laugh. That's all."

"Take it from me, Trey. A woman prefers to laugh instead of cry. If I don't make Ros laugh at least a couple times during the day, then I start worrying. I know I'm not doing something right."

The idea of Chandler not keeping Roslyn happy was ridiculous. The woman was crazy in love with him and he with her. And they had the children to prove it.

"When it comes to your family, you know what you're doing. It's different for you than it is for me. You had a great dad. He worshipped his children and his wife. My dad—well, he tried. But being married and having a kid just wasn't his thing. He's better off single. And I'm a chip off the old block."

From the corner of his eye, Trey could see Chandler shaking his head. "You're wrong, Trey. You don't want to be like your father. That's why you didn't go with him to Montana all those years ago when your parents divorced. It's why you're still here and not up there with him. You view life differently than him."

Chandler had that much right. Trey loved his father, but he didn't want to live out his life in a bunkhouse with a crew of men who didn't care if they ever had a home or family of their own.

"Maybe so," Trey said, then hoping to direct their conversation elsewhere, he asked, "Has anything new been happening with solving your father's murder case? Sorry, I guess I shouldn't have said murder. But I don't know what else to call it."

"No need to be sorry. Naming it something else won't make it any less ugly." Heaving out a breath, Chandler turned his gaze toward the passenger window. "The situation is in a holding pattern right now. There's not much going on with the case. Joe and Connor are still waiting for Ginny Patterson to set up a meeting with them. Apparently, she has an abusive husband and doesn't want him to know about it."

Joseph Hollister was Chandler's younger brother and had worked more than a decade as a deputy sheriff for Yavapai County. Over the years, Connor Murphy, his friend and fellow deputy, had been helping Joseph dig into the cause of Joel Hollister's death. Together, the two deputies had recently discovered a major lead in the form of a woman named Ginny Patterson.

"You really believe this Ginny woman has important information about your dad's death?" Trey asked.

Lifting his hat a few inches off his head, Chandler raked a hand through his hair as though he wanted to plow the whole situation out of his brain.

"She has to be the key. From what we can gather from the personal notes of the late Sheriff Maddox, Dad was spotted with this woman several times at the Phoenix livestock auction. Mom even found an old day planner of Dad's where he'd penciled in a reminder to meet her, but the meeting didn't take place. He was killed the day before. Joe and Connor learned that shortly afterward she suddenly quit her job at the auction barn. And from what my brother says, she was a poor woman then and is still living in poverty."

"Could be coincidence about the meeting and quitting the job," Trey said.

"Could be. But it's too coincidental for me to swallow."

Trey thought about that for a moment before he asked, "Does your brother, Joe, and his partner, Connor, think this woman could've killed Joel? Or helped someone commit the crime? Frankly, Doc, what would be the motive? If the woman needed money, kidnapping for ransom would've been more logical."

"You're right. And that could've been the initial plan," Chandler said. "We all have our theories on the matter."

Trey shook his head. "Well, I don't know that I'd have the patience to wait around on this woman to decide when and where she wants to talk. What if she gets it in her head to run? Your link would go missing."

"She hasn't run in all these years since Dad died. Not likely she will now. Besides, we've waited this long for the truth. We can wait a little longer."

Trey glanced at him. "I'm not anything close to being a lawman or private investigator, but am I stupid to think she could use the phone? Maybe somewhere away from her husband? What's wrong with that form of communication?"

"There's too much that needs to be discussed. And Uncle Gil says you have to be face-to-face when you interrogate someone. To read the nuances in expressions—that sort of thing. Anyway, they need to see firsthand that they're actually speaking with Ginny Patterson."

"That's true. And your dad's brother was a detective for the Phoenix Police Department for, what, thirty years or more? He ought to know."

"Yes. Uncle Gil has been a godsend to the family

in more ways than one," Chandler admitted. "Especially for Mom. Before he moved back to Three Rivers, she'd really sunk into a dark place."

Trey said, "I never noticed Maureen acting like she was in a funk. But then, anytime I'm ever on the ranch, she's always working—helping the hands do something, or helping Holt with the yearlings. But now that I think about it, she has seemed a lot more chipper since Gil come home."

"Come home." Chandler thoughtfully repeated the words. "Funny how natural it seems to have Uncle Gil around now. I'll be honest, Trey, in the beginning I wasn't sure how I felt about Mom falling in love again—especially with Dad's brother. Actually, thinking of her with any man, other than Dad, seemed weird to me. But Dad is gone and life goes on. Mom deserves to have love in her life again."

The highway was cutting through a plateau of red rock and shell. Scrubby pines and twisted juniper clung to the steep cliffs, while ahead of them, a line of bald mountains rose above the desert floor. Even though Trey had seen this area thousands of times, he never grew tired of traveling this particular highway. Today, however, he wasn't noticing the beauty of the landscape. Chandler had given him too much to think about.

"Yeah," he said pensively. "Like Granny. She deserves to be loved, too. Here lately, I've had to remind myself of that."

Chandler looked at him. "Why? Does Virgie have a fella now?"

"I think it's more like he has her," Trey said wryly. "He's asked her to marry him and she hasn't turned him down. That tells me she's thinking hard about this guy."

"Hmm. Sounds serious. Do you know him?"

A few days ago, Chandler's question would've drawn a curse word from Trey. But something had happened to him since his visit with Virgie. And his changed attitude had everything to do with Nicole; he could admit that much. She was making him look at everything and everyone around him in a different way. Did that mean he might be falling in love with her? No! Not that. She'd just made him a bit more open-minded, that's all, he assured himself.

"I know him. You do, too. It's Harley Hutchison. The farmer who raises melons over by Aguila."

Trey expected Chandler to turn a shocked look on him. Instead, he merely nodded.

"Last time I saw Harley was when he brought that nanny with a ruptured teat to the clinic," Chandler recalled. "I kept her for a few days of treatment. Nice guy. You ought to be really happy for Virgie."

"I'm trying to warm up to the idea," Trey conceded, then asked, "You don't think he's too young or, uh, too much of a man for Granny?"

Chandler laughed. "If Virgie doesn't think he's too young and Harley doesn't think she's too old, then more power to them. That's what I say." Stretching his arm across the back of the seat, he turned so that he was looking at Trey head-on. "Your problem is that you've never been in love."

"Damn it, I don't—"

"No. Don't start reminding me of Rhonda or Lacey again. You weren't in love with either of those women. If you had really been in love, you would've gone through hell and high water to make it work. But you didn't."

"Hellfire! You think I deliberately chased those women away?"

Chandler groaned. "No. But you didn't make much effort to keep either of them around, did you? Let me tell you, Trey, when you do finally fall in love, you're going to know it. Because nothing else in the world will matter except having *her* in your life. And you'll do whatever you have to do to make sure that happens."

Trey could admit, at least to himself, that he wanted Nicole's company. But he couldn't imagine having her in his life on a permanent basis. What would it be like to wake up with her lying next to him? How would it feel to see her sleepy eyes open and rest lovingly on his face?

The questions caused a lump to form in his throat. When it finally eased enough for him to speak, he said, "Aw, Doc, you know me. I'm a confirmed bachelor. I need my space. I need to be able to go to the Fandango anytime I get ready."

"Fandango, hell," Chandler muttered. "That'll keep you warm in your old age."

Trey fixed his gaze on the highway and didn't say another word until they reached the Bar 40.

Hours later, the waiting room at Hollister Animal Clinic was finally empty, and Nicole was organizing the work on her desk as the clock wound down to closing time. With two minutes to go, the phone rang and she didn't hesitate to answer.

After the client gave her a brief explanation of what she needed, Nicole said, "Doctor Hollister reserves Thursday mornings for feline spaying and neutering, Mrs. Roberts. I have one vacancy left for this coming Thursday if you—" The woman interrupted with a frantic protest, forcing Nicole to pause. At the same time the woman's voice was rattling in her ear, she sensed a presence behind her and swiveled her chair just enough to see Loretta giving her a look that said she was thanking her lucky stars she was a bookkeeper instead of a receptionist.

Giving her coworker a grin, Nicole rolled her eyes helplessly before focusing her attention back on the caller. "Yes, on occasion Doctor Hollister will make exceptions. I can ask him and get back to you tomorrow," Nicole suggested. "Presently, he's out on a house call and won't be back before closing hours."

Thankfully, the woman agreed, and after Nicole had carefully jotted down her name and number, she hung up the phone, then turned her chair so that she was facing Loretta head-on.

The young woman had dark green eyes and vibrant red hair that curled upon her shoulders. Several inches taller than Nicole, she had a statuesque build that curved in all the right places. Nicole was still wondering why the woman didn't have a fiancé or even a steady boyfriend, but apparently from what Nicole could gather, Loretta preferred living a solitary life.

"Everyone thinks they should be an exception to the rule, right?" she asked.

Nicole chuckled. "Not everyone. But probably the majority. At least the woman was very nice about it. And she did have a legitimate reason for needing another day besides Thursday."

Loretta leaned her hip against the edge of Nicole's desk. "Nicci, you're too nice for your own good. No matter how hard you try, you can't make everyone happy. Although, I'll have to say you've made Trey one happy fellow," she added slyly.

The mention of Trey's name caused Nicole's heart to break into a tap dance against her rib cage. "What are you talking about? Trey is always a happy guy. Since I've started work here, I've never seen him unhappy."

"That's my point," Loretta said, then laughed at

the confused look on Nicole's face. "Oh, Nicci, I'm teasing. Well, kind of teasing," she admitted. "I ran into Trey yesterday in the break room. He was telling me you've turned into a regular little miner."

"Oh. He did? Well, he's exaggerating. I struggled trying to get the hang of swirling the water out of the pan without losing all the gravel," Nicole told her.

Loretta shook her head. "You must've done something right. You found gold. Do you have any idea how long I tried before I found a few flakes? Probably twenty trips."

Nicole hadn't said much to her coworkers about her and Trey's panning expedition last Sunday. For one thing, she figured the women wouldn't be thinking of the prospecting trip in terms of searching for gold. All of them, including Roslyn, would be thinking of romance.

Well, your friends would be right, wouldn't they, Nicci? Spending that time with Trey had been about being near him, savoring each touch and kiss he'd given her, rather than digging for a golden treasure.

"We had good luck. But actually, it was even nicer to be enjoying the outdoors. I didn't do much of that in Fort Worth," she said. "Honestly, I was mostly an indoor girl."

Loretta nodded. "Roslyn has told us before about her life back in Texas. She said you two made trips to the malls and theaters and concerts—things like that. It sounds exciting. Especially when you compare it to scooping up gravel out of a creek bed."

Nicole closed her appointment book and switched off a lamp sitting on one corner of the desk. "Not really, Loretta. I've had more fun since I moved here than I've had in a long, long time."

Loretta fixed her with a pointed look. "Is that because of Trey?"

She'd not expected the woman to ask her such a blunt question, and for a moment she floundered as she wondered how to answer. Finally, she decided on the truth.

"Yes, I suppose it is." The soft note in her voice revealed the emotions he evoked in her, and though she tried to clear them away with a little cough, she knew Loretta had already heard them.

"The last time I remember Trey dating anyone steadily was several years ago. We all thought he was going to get married. He never told us what happened to end it, but I'm sure Doc knows the whole story."

Nicole often wondered if Trey had ever loved or endured a broken heart. Now she knew, and the fact tore at something deep within her. She didn't want to think of Trey anguishing over a woman. Not any more than she wanted to think of him making love to one.

Rising to her feet, Nicole said, "Well, that's really none of my business."

Loretta continued to scrutinize Nicole's face.

"Why, Nicci, you've really fallen for the guy. Haven't you?"

"You're jumping to ridiculous conclusions. I've not known Trey long enough for something like that."

"Really? Whatever happened to love at first sight?" the bookkeeper asked.

"That's totally not sensible."

Laughing, Loretta asked, "Who gave you the idea that there was anything sensible about love?"

Nicole was trying to come up with a logical reply to that when Cybil entered the waiting room. Seeing it was empty, she walked over to the counter that separated the customers from Nicole's work area.

"Looks like we're all finished," Cybil said. "Are you two girls ready to lock up and go home?"

"I'm more than ready. My washing machine is trying to lie down and die. I need to go by the appliance place and price a new one or ask Malcom if he can fix mine without it costing me a fortune," Loretta said, then gave Nicole a conspiring wink. "See you two tomorrow."

Loretta left the room, and Nicole gathered up her handbag and the thin jacket she'd worn over her sundress early this morning.

"I'll lock the front door and we'll go out the back," Cybil told her. "Doc and Trey came in a few minutes ago. They can finish locking up whenever they get ready to leave."

Just hearing that Trey was actually in the building

caused Nicole's heart to take an excited leap. She'd not had a chance to talk with him since they parted late Sunday evening, and she'd missed him terribly. Several times, she'd come close to picking up the phone and texting him, or even walking up to the treatment barns to say hello. But she'd told herself that chasing after the man wasn't the answer. If he'd already forgotten about those kisses they'd shared in the arroyo, then she needed to forget them, too.

"Yes, I'm ready," she told Cybil, and after switching off the overhead fluorescent light, she joined the woman out in the hallway.

The two women walked side by side past the treatment rooms and on toward the back of the building where a large recovery area held the caged animals that needed to remain at the hospital for extended care. Along the way, the loud sounds of barking dogs and meowing cats carried down the wide corridor.

"What a day," Cybil said with a weary sigh. "I'm so tired I barely know my own name."

"It's Cybil. Just in case you're wondering," Nicole joked.

Laughing, Cybil wrapped one arm around the back of Nicole's shoulders and squeezed. "Thanks for reminding me. And just think, we have the pleasure of doing this all over again tomorrow."

Nicole laughed along with her. "I wouldn't miss it for anything."

A few feet ahead, the door to Chandler's office stood partially open, and she could hear the two men's voices drifting out from the room. Even though she was longing to see Trey, she didn't pause to look in, or say good-night. No doubt the pair were discussing work, and she didn't want to be a nuisance by interrupting.

Outside the back door of the clinic, the two women said their good-nights and walked on to their cars, which were parked on opposite sides of the graveled lot.

Nicole had just opened the driver's door and tossed in her purse when she heard the sound of crunching footsteps behind her, and then Trey's voice called out.

"Nicci, wait up!"

Her heart beating fast, she glanced over her shoulder to see him trotting up to her.

"Hello, Trey."

He was smiling at her, and the smile she gave him in return was so wide she could feel it stretching her face. So much for being subtle, she thought.

"I saw you walk by the office and I, uh, wanted to catch you before you left," he explained.

"Was there something you wanted to tell me?"

He reached for her hand and smoothed it between the two of his. "Just that I've been so busy since we started back to work Monday that I haven't had time to go to the front of the clinic and talk with you.

I—uh—didn't want you to think I was deliberately avoiding you."

The sun had already dipped behind the western horizon and shadowed the parking area at the side of the building, but Nicci suddenly felt as though bright sunshine were pouring down on her.

"I didn't think you were trying to avoid me. Remember, I make the appointments. I know how busy you are." Her gaze met his, and she instinctively stepped a bit closer. "I have missed you, though."

The smile on his lips eased to a tender slant. "I've missed you, too. That's another thing I wanted to tell you."

Feeling an overwhelming urge to touch him, she placed her free hand on his forearm. "I've been thinking that we—uh—should have dinner together again. What are you doing tonight? Is it urgent that you go straight home?"

His brows lifted slightly as he glanced down at his soiled jeans and shirt. "No. It's not urgent. But I can't go out like this."

"I wasn't thinking about going out," she told him. "We can have dinner at my place. I'll go by the deli and pick up something. You've not seen my house yet. I'd like to show it to you."

His eyes lifted back to her face, and judging by his expression, it was obvious to Nicole that her invitation had surprised him. Actually, she'd surprised herself. She was continually telling herself that she needed to sit back and wait for Trey to do the asking. But she was quickly learning that he was far from the forward type—at least, with her he wasn't taking the lead. She didn't know if that was because he felt unsure about having a relationship with her, or whether he'd rather they remain friends.

When he didn't immediately respond, she quickly added, "It's okay if you'd rather not, Trey. I'm sure you're tired and you probably want to get home and rest."

He suddenly chuckled. "Rest. What's that? I don't need rest."

She let out a pent-up breath. "Does that mean you want to come?"

"Sure. I'd like it—a lot," he said softly. "I have a few things here to wrap up, but I can be there in thirty minutes. Is that okay?"

Impulsively, she rose on her toes and kissed his cheek. "It's perfect. I'll see you then." She started to climb into her car, then remembered he didn't know where she lived. "Oh, I'd better give you my address so you can find me."

Reaching into the car, she fished a pen and scrap of paper from her purse and jotted down the address.

"And just in case you have trouble finding it, the house is pale yellow with brown trim and the yard has a chain-link fence. You'll see my car parked beneath the carport," Nicole added.

"No worries. I'll put your address into my phone. It has a navigational app. I'll see you in a bit."

He jogged off in the direction of the treatment barn, and Nicole hopped into the car and practically threw gravel as she hurried out of the parking lot.

She had thirty minutes to stop by the deli and pick out something yummy for dinner and then get home and make herself look presentable. That was hardly enough time to take pains with her appearance, but she didn't care. She was going to be with Trey again and that was all it took to send her spirits soaring.

Chapter Eight

Trey usually kept a set of clean clothes in a locker at the clinic just in case he might need a change. But a few weeks ago, he'd used the clothes and hadn't bothered to replace them.

Now, as he walked onto Nicole's porch, he looked ruefully down at his chambray shirt and blue jeans. Both were covered with sweat, dust and dark patches where cow manure had splattered and dried. Maybe she wouldn't notice the stains too much, he thought, but the smell might knock her for a loop.

He was in the process of lifting the small brass knocker on the door when it swung open and the precious sight of Nicole's smiling face made him forget all about his disheveled appearance and the fact that he smelled like a bull pen.

"Hi, Trey!" She pushed the door wider and gestured for him to enter. "Welcome to my house."

Stepping past her, he found himself standing in a small foyer furnished with a brass hall tree and a potted cactus with a pair of red blooms in front of a single long window. But his attention was hardly on his surroundings. Not when she looked like a sweet dream in a blue checked sundress and her hair wound in a loose knot atop her head.

All he wanted to do was pull her into his arms and kiss her senseless. Instead, he stood patiently to one side while she dealt with the door. But when he heard the lock click, the reality that they were entirely alone sent a spurt of panic through him. How was he going to keep his hands to himself and his mind on something other than making love to her?

She didn't give him time to come up with a strategy as she quickly looped her arm through his and urged him out of the foyer.

"Other than Roslyn, you're the first guest I've had since I moved in," she said as they strolled into a rectangular-shaped living room. "Actually, one of my neighbors came as far as the porch to say hello. I guess I could count him."

"Him?"

She smiled coyly up at him. "Mr. Bains. He's eighty and a widower. He retired here in Wickenburg so he could play golf year-round. Sometimes I see him leaving with his clubs as I'm leaving for work."

Trey chuckled. "Now he's the kind of man Granny needs. Elderly and safe."

She gave his arm a playful pinch. "You leave your grandmother alone. She wants passion—not snoring."

Yeah, Harley was probably capable of giving Virgie plenty of that, Trey thought crossly.

You need to wake up, Trey. You have a problem with Harley because you don't have the backbone to be like him. Because you don't have the guts to go after the woman you want. Because you turn into a trembling coward when you think about marriage.

Fighting the taunting voice inside his head, he asked, "How do you know what Granny wants? You've never met her."

Her laugh was a little wicked. "From what you've said about her, she's a woman who enjoys life. That tells me plenty. As for Mr. Bains snoring, he has a hefty paunch. I'm guessing he raises the rafters every night."

Slanting her a wry look, he patted a hand against his abdomen. "I'd better start watching what I eat. I don't want to start raising the rafters."

Chuckling, she gestured toward the furniture grouped into a cozy U in the middle of the room. The couch and love seat were upholstered in dark red fabric, while the chairs were a deep moss green.

Brown leather hassocks were positioned in front of both chairs, while colorful throw pillows dotted all the plush furniture.

"Go ahead and be honest," she said. "All I need to add is a decorated tree and it would look like Christmas."

"Nothing wrong with that. I like it," he said truthfully.

"Thanks. Comfort was my main objective." She gestured toward the walls, which were painted a light gray color. "I don't have many pictures or wall hangings put up yet, and I still need a few scatter rugs, but its slowly coming together."

The room looked like a real home, he thought. Was that because it had a woman's touch? Or because he was standing next to Nicole, imagining himself as a permanent fixture in her life?

He cleared his throat. "If the rest of the house looks like this, then you've been busy."

She reached for his hand. "Come on," she said. "I'm sure you're tired and hungry. Let's go eat and I'll show you the other rooms later."

She led him through an arched doorway and into an angular space that intersected with two separate hallways shooting off to the left and right. Straight ahead was a pair of slatted swinging doors.

He followed her through the doors and into a kitchen with a long row of windows facing a backyard, plenty of white cabinets and a round pine table with matching chairs. A shaded lamp swung over the table, while a light over a gas range illuminated the work area.

Releasing his hand, she crossed over to the cabinet counter. "I got enchiladas and sides to go with them. I hope you like Mexican food. Otherwise, you might have to settle for a peanut butter sandwich."

"Don't worry," he assured her. "I love Mexican food."

She opened a microwave and pulled out a glass dish. "Go ahead and have a seat," she told him. "I'll bring everything over."

"I can help," he offered.

Shaking her head, she glanced in his direction. "Thanks, but you're my guest."

Is that how she considered him? Just a guest dropping by for supper and a bit of conversation? Trey wanted to be more than that. He wanted to be her everything. He wanted the right to hold and kiss her, make love to her. He wanted her to belong to him and him to belong to her.

He wasn't sure when or how he'd reached that conclusion. Or what he intended to do about it. He only knew that when she'd opened the door and invited him into her home, he'd felt happier than he'd ever been in his life.

"Okay, if you're so intent on spoiling me, I'll sit." He started toward the table, then paused midstride.

"I wasn't thinking, Nicci. I washed my hands before I left the clinic, but I think I ought to wash again."

"Oh, sorry, I'm not a very good hostess. I should've shown you to the bathroom." She placed the dish of enchiladas on the table, then motioned for him to follow her out of the kitchen. "It's right down the hallway."

Outside the swinging doors, she turned left and they immediately walked past an open doorway on the right.

"The dining room is in there," she explained, gesturing toward the doorway. "But I didn't think we needed to use it tonight."

He chuckled. "The way I look, I'm surprised you let me in the house. Much less into the dining room."

"Nonsense. You look like a man who's been working outside with his hands. That's very sexy."

Trey came close to stumbling. "I—uh—I'll take your word for it," he said sheepishly.

She laughed softly. "Trey, you have to be the most modest, guileless man I've ever met."

"Is that supposed to be a compliment?" he asked.

By now they'd reached a doorway on the left and she stopped and turned to him. The gnawing hunger in his stomach was instantly forgotten as her hands flattened against his chest and pushed their way upward.

"It's very much a compliment," she whispered.

His gaze collided with hers and then, all at once,

he was struggling to breathe. There was something in her gray eyes conveying far more than her words, even more than the pressure of her fingers wrapping urgently over the ridge of his shoulders.

"Then I should be thanking you," he murmured.

She rose up on her tiptoes and angled her mouth to his. "My very same thoughts."

Trey didn't waste time wondering why she was offering her lips to him, or even why the look in her eyes told him she wanted him in the most basic way a woman could want a man. The why of it no longer mattered to Trey. He was tired of trying to figure out her motives and even more tired of trying to resist the fire she built in him.

When his lips came down on hers, she let out a welcoming groan and curled both arms around his neck. Trey responded by wrapping his arms around her waist and tugging her body tightly against his.

The thought to keep the kiss gentle and contained lasted for about two seconds. After that, the contact of their lips turned to a reckless hunger that shot a hot blaze straight to his loins.

Along the way, Trey fought to hold on to his senses, but the taste of her lips was like sipping from a fountain of wine. By the time she opened her mouth to invite his tongue inside, he was desperate to be inside her and feel her warm body yielding to his.

The need for air finally forced their heads to part, and as they both sucked in several long breaths, Trey could feel his heart pounding like a sledgehammer against his rib cage. Beneath his hands, he could feel her shoulders trembling, and the fact that he'd had that much effect on her stunned him.

"Nicci, I—"

She suddenly looked up at him, and Trey forgot the words he was about to speak. Instead, he was taking note of how her eyes had darkened to a stormy gray and her puffy lips had turned to a deep shade of rose. The dimly lit hallway created shadows across her cheeks and chin, and before he realized what he was doing, his fingertips were tracing the flickering shapes upon her soft skin.

"I wondered how long I was going to have to wait for you to do that," she whispered in a raw voice. "I was beginning to think you didn't want me."

He groaned. "Want you? Nicci, if I wanted you any more than I do right now, it would kill me."

His throat was so tight it sounded like he was choking. She must've recognized the agony in his voice, because her palm was suddenly resting against his cheek and her soft gaze was delving into his.

"You're worried. Why?"

He groaned a second time. "This might be a huge mistake. I don't want to hurt you. I don't want you to hurt me. Maybe we need to forget—"

"Forget what?" she interrupted in a hoarse, shaky voice. "How we make each other feel? Forget what it's like when we touch each other, kiss each other? Maybe you can forget, but I'm past that point."

The urgency in her words was all the persuasion he needed to crush his mouth back onto hers, and as he gathered her into his arms, he realized he was also past the point of forgetting. All he wanted now was to let himself touch and feel and savor these moments of making love to her.

When the kiss finally ended, she grabbed his hand and tugged him on down the hallway and through a partially open door on the right.

Beyond the slightly opened blinds at the window, he could see the last bit of daylight rapidly disappearing. Shadows slanted across a queen-size four-poster bed and a nearby dresser, the top of which was scattered with perfume bottles and other feminine items. As she led him toward the bed, he noticed a dressing screen stretched across one corner of the room. A few garments were tossed over the top, while on the bed, a blue-and-white comforter was rumpled from where she'd sat on the edge of the mattress. Above it all, the scent of her perfume lingered faintly in the air and pushed his swirling senses to an even drunker state.

By the time they reached a spot near the bedside, she began to unsnap his shirt. Trey could only wonder if she'd pulled him into some sort of exotic dream where he didn't belong.

Shaking his head with confusion, he said, "This is too nice. I'm not fit for this room—or for you."

"That's crazy thinking," she murmured.

Each snap she pulled apart sent more muddling fog into Trey's brain. "I, uh, don't belong here." The front pieces of his shirt parted, and as her fingertips brushed his skin, his breath lodged somewhere deep in his throat. "Maybe I—should go get in the shower. And give you—time to think."

Seeming to ignore his words, she pushed the garment off his shoulders and down his arms.

"I don't need time to analyze you or this. And you're not about to go anywhere." Leaning forward, she pressed her lips to his bare chest, then proceeded to scatter a row of kisses down his breastbone. Once she reached the bottom of it, she made a sharp turn and directed her attention to his left nipple. Using the tip of her tongue to circle the flat brown flesh, she whispered, "I want you just as you are. Salty and sexy and oh—so—good."

While she continued to slide her parted lips over his skin, Trey thrust fingers into her hair and held the tips against her scalp. She had to stop, he thought desperately. If she didn't, he was going to break into a thousand useless pieces.

"Sweet Nicci," he said thickly. "Let me look at you—touch you—every inch of you."

His mouth dropped to her bare shoulder, and as he gently sunk his teeth into her soft skin, his fingers pulled down the zipper at the back of her dress. When the tiny straps slid off her shoulders, the rest of the garment followed, until the fabric pooled around her feet.

Trey stepped back, and as his gaze took in the pink lace bra and tiny matching panties, she said, "I'm not much of a curvy girl. I hope you're not disappointed."

Disappointed? Didn't she realize that having her standing here like this, offering herself to him, was nearly as incredible as him reaching into the sky and touching a star?

With a shake of his head, he wrapped his hands around the sides of her waist and marveled that his fingers very nearly spanned the distance.

"Don't you know how beautiful you are? How desirable?" His hands slipped up her back until they reached her hair. After fishing out the pins, the knot fell and the thick strawberry-blond curtain swung down around her face and onto her shoulders. He sniffed its lovely scent before sliding a thumb beneath her chin and lifting her mouth to his.

This time he held the kiss to a slow, seductive search, but instead of tempering the fire that was growing between them, it grew to mammoth portions. Soon her tongue was thrusting boldly between his teeth, demanding he give her more.

A tidal wave of desire washed over him, nearly drowning him with swirling heat. He felt his erection pushing at the fly of his jeans and heard a loud rush of blood in his ears. At the same time, he realized she was groaning and fumbling with his belt.

Stepping back, he gently took hold of her hands and placed them at her sides. "It's a tricky buckle," he said thickly. "I'll do it."

She sat down on the edge of the bed and waited while he rapidly dealt with his boots and jeans. When he was finally stripped down to nothing but a pair of black boxers, he joined her on the bed and, with his hands on her shoulders, gently eased her down onto the mattress.

Lying face-to-face, he rested his forehead against hers. "I didn't know this was going to happen," he said, then groaned as he realized how inane that sounded. "I mean—I thought it could—but I didn't know. I was hoping—not planning. Hell, I'm not making sense!"

She wrapped her arm around his waist and snugged the front of her body next to his. "You're making perfect sense to me. I hadn't planned on this happening tonight, either. But when we kissed—" Her sigh brushed against his cheek. "I'm glad it's happening. You'd probably have a red face if I told you how long I've wanted this."

"I think I'm blushing all over," he admitted. "And I'm going to quit asking myself why you want me. I'm just very, very glad that you do."

He didn't wait for her to reply. Instead, he closed

his lips over hers, and immediately her mouth opened beneath his. Her arm moved from around his waist to slip a tight circle around his neck.

In a matter of seconds, the kiss turned into another fiery exchange, and the need to be inside her caused his loins to ache, his jaw to clench with what little restraint he had left.

Eventually, the need to have her totally naked forced his head back from hers, and he turned his attention to removing the lacy lingerie. Once the bra was unhooked and tossed aside, he curved his forefingers over the waistband of the bikini panties and slid the scrap of lace down her silky legs until the fabric dangled off her toes and fell to the floor.

With a hand cupping the weight of each little breast, he studied the pale pink nipples. "Perfect," he whispered. "Everything about you is perfect."

Her eyelids fluttered open and she smiled up at him. "The room is full of shadows. You're seeing a blurred version of me."

Odd that she should say that, Trey thought. For the first time in his life, he felt as though he was seeing her and his surroundings with absolute clarity. He didn't belong here. He could see that, even if she couldn't. But for now, it didn't matter. Tomorrow and reality would arrive soon enough.

"Wrong, sweet Nicci, I'm seeing all of you," he murmured. "And I want everything I'm seeing."

"Then please don't close your eyes, Trey. Because all of me is what I want to give you."

A hot lump suddenly filled his throat, and to hide the sudden onslaught of emotions, he dropped his head and buried his face between her breasts. Beneath his lips, her skin was like velvety smooth cream, tempting him to lick and

taste. When he gently closed his teeth around one nipple, he felt her hand push its way past the waistband of his boxers, then on downward to his throbbing manhood.

The delicate touch of her fingers very nearly sent him over the edge, and with a great groan of resistance, he brushed away her exploring hand and practically leaped off the bed.

A confused frown on her face, she sat up. "What's wrong?"

The concern in her voice made him wonder if the last man she'd made love to had been some sort of superman with a will of iron. Or was she so innocent she didn't realize she'd been about to end everything before it ever got started.

Turning his back to her, he found his wallet and fished out a condom. "No! I just can't handle wanting you *this* much! That's all."

"Oh."

His fingers fumbled as he urgently attempted to roll on the protective sheath. When he finally managed to finish the task, he turned back to see she was watching him through half-closed eyes. The come-hither expression on her face was like nothing he'd ever seen on a woman before, and the fire that was already burning inside him launched into a raging blaze.

Holding out her arms to him, she murmured softly, "Come here."

He rejoined her on the bed and quickly positioned himself over her. As his knee slid between her thighs, she looked up at him and Trey thought he would drown in her gray eyes. Along with desire swimming in the luminous depths, he saw so much tenderness and caring that his boggled brain couldn't take it all in.

"Nicci—sweetheart. You're incredible."

The words barely made it past his tight throat, but they weren't so garbled that she didn't hear him. One hand snared a hold on the back of his neck and drew his head down to hers. Then with his forehead resting against hers, he lowered his hips and entered her with one smooth thrust.

Before Trey connected their bodies, Nicole believed she was ready for him. She thought she knew exactly what to expect from him and herself. But she couldn't have been more wrong.

The moment he entered her, she felt the hair practically lift from her scalp. Her fingers curled into her palms and the air in her lungs whooshed past her lips with such a force it sounded like a balloon let loose to fly across the room.

As he began to slowly and carefully move inside her, she wondered if he'd carried her off to an unworldly place where there was only soft, heated space and the sounds of their breathing.

His skin felt as hot as a sunbaked rock and tasted as salty as the sea against her tongue. While her hands made a roaming search of his muscled body, her mouth nibbled its way across his wide chest, down the corded arms and back to the strong column of his neck. And all the while, their hips moved in unison, faster and deeper, until the bond between them was so complete she wasn't sure where her body stopped and his began. She only knew that he was all she would ever want. Ever need.

Time continued to tick on as the two of them made love in the darkening room, but Nicole didn't have any idea of where the hands were on the bedside clock. She was aware only of Trey and the wild desire he was creating with each caress, each kiss, each plunge of his hips. If the night lasted forever, it wouldn't be long enough.

But nothing this good could last that long. The thought raced desperately through her mind and made her even more frantic to hold him close, to feel the rapid thump of his heart banging against her breast and have his hard-driving thrusts lift her higher and higher.

Somewhere deep inside her, coiled pressure began to build until she was certain it was going to spring open and shatter her body into a million pieces. She fought to remain in control, but Trey wouldn't allow it. His lips swallowed hers up, his hands clamped around the inner part of her thighs and lifted her lower body to an angle that left no space between them.

His strained grunts drifted to her ears, and then she heard nothing but the sound of her own heart as it hammered out a euphoric crescendo.

Suddenly she was crying his name and clutching his shoulders as she felt herself whirling, falling end over end into a vortex from which she never wanted to escape. At the same time, he buried his face in the curve of her neck while shudders of relief racked his body.

What was he doing here? How had this happened? Even before he rolled onto his side and opened his eyes to see Nicole's face lying next to his, the questions were revolving around in Trey's head. Now as he studied her soft features dampened with sweat, he was even more confused.

From the moment he'd walked into Chandler's office and laid eyes on her, he'd thought the most he could ever be to her was a co-worker. At best, a friend. The idea that they would wind up as lovers was like a page out of a fantasy book. This proved that dreams did come true. But did they last? That was the question that truly haunted him.

He was trying to shut out what it all meant, trying not to think about tomorrow, when her eyes fluttered open and the corners of her mouth tilted upward.

"My darling, Trey."

The whispered words were followed by the trace of her fingertips against his cheek. And because his heart was so full, he closed his eyes and brought the palm of her hand to his lips.

"Nicci."

Her name was all he could manage to say, but she didn't appear to expect more. Still smiling, she scooted closer and pillowed her head upon his shoulder.

"Forgive me for being a terrible hostess. I've kept you from dinner when you must be starving."

Laughing, he said in a teasing voice, "Well, bringing me into your bed instead of giving me a plate of enchiladas was kind of rude. Am I supposed to exist on you and air alone?"

"That is the idea." She made a purring noise. "But I won't let you starve. I'll heat everything again."

Trey reached for the corner of the comforter and pulled the cover over both of them. "There's no hurry." He slipped a hand down her arm, then on to the curve of her hip. "And lying here next to you feels too good to move."

"Mmm. I'm not sure I *can* move."

He rested his cheek against the top of her head. "I don't think you understand how you've made me feel."

She pressed a kiss on his chin. "Happy, I hope."

Happy wasn't the word for it, Trey thought. *Euphoric* was a closer description, but even that seemed tame considering the wild trip his emotions had taken as he'd made love to her.

Made love. He'd quit making love to a woman ever since Lacey had moved out of his life. No, that was hardly the truth, he thought. Because at some point during the past half hour he'd discovered that, before tonight, he'd never made love. For all these years, he'd only been performing the sex act. This thing with Nicole was entirely different. She'd caused an upheaval in his very heart and soul.

Even so, he was too cowardly to admit the truth. The most he could do was nuzzle his nose against her hair and murmur, "Yes. Very happy."

She nestled her cheek in the middle of his chest and wrapped her arm across his waist. The tender reaction had Trey wondering if this was how a king felt with all his treasures laid out before him.

"I guess by now you're thinking you've been chased and cornered."

He grunted with amusement. "No woman has ever chased me, Nicci."

"Until me," she said impishly. "I don't care to admit it. I mean, maybe it wasn't all-out chasing, but

I wanted to make sure you understood that I liked you—a lot."

"That's the mystery. What you've ever seen in me," he said.

"I've wondered the same thing about you. I'm not exactly a prize. But here you are with me anyway. And I'm so glad you are."

The hand at his side moved to his rib cage, and as she hugged him tightly, a weird pressure began to build in his chest and spread to his throat. He tried to swallow the feeling away before he took her chin between his thumb and forefinger and tilted her face up to his.

"Do you understand how special you are? How beautiful?"

Smiling wanly, she touched her fingertips to his cheek, and Trey couldn't help but think this was how it must feel to have an angel in his arms.

"There are plenty of beautiful women in the world," she said pointedly.

He stroked his fingers through the long hair lying against her back. "I haven't seen that many around here."

She chuckled. "I don't believe that. Fort Worth was full of them."

"Is that why you left? You didn't want to be a little fish in a big ocean?"

She playfully pinched a bit of flesh at the side of

his waist. "Is that what you think? That I need to be the center of attention?"

A chuckle rumbled out of him. "No. I was only teasing." He rubbed his cheek against her temple as his thoughts quickly sobered. "But I would like to know the real reason why you left Texas. You must've had a nice life there."

She let out a weighty sigh. "I did have a nice life there. I think I told you that Dad has always made plenty of money. And when it came to me and my brother, he and Mom never held back. We always had a nice home and most everything we wanted."

"Were you living with them when you moved here?"

"Yes. But that's a whole other story."

Her voice was full of regret and sadness, and Trey was suddenly remembering back to that first day he'd met her at the clinic and he'd walked into the break room to find her sniffing back tears. Had her distress been over her parents or letting go of the man who'd wanted to marry her?

"Would it bother you to share it with me?" he asked, even though better judgment told him that the less he knew about her, the easier it would be for him whenever she dumped him. And she would dump him, he thought ruefully. There was no doubt in his mind about that.

"It wouldn't bother me. Maybe with someone else it would, but not with you. Because I think—" She reached up and traced a fingertip down the side of his neck. "Because you're not judgmental like most folks are."

Trey suddenly felt like a snake, forked tongue and all. He'd already judged her as a woman who'd spend a bit of pleasurable time with him and then move on.

"You have me confused with someone else," he told her, then urged, "but tell me about your parents anyway."

Propping her head up with her hand, she studied his face. "They were married for twenty-six years when Dad went a little crazy and had an affair with a much younger woman. He thought he wanted a divorce so he'd be free to marry again. And even though it very nearly killed her, Mom gave him what he wanted and he moved away from Fort Worth."

He frowned. "Your parents divorced?"

Nodding, she said, "That's when everything went to hell. I wasn't living with my parents at that time. I had moved out several years prior and was living in an apartment close to my job, and I had spent lots of hours and money furnishing it just the way I wanted. But my parents' marital crisis forced me to give up my home and move in with Mom. You see, losing Dad caused her to have a mental breakdown. Angela—that's my mom—was in such bad shape she couldn't even take care of herself. I had to do most everything for her. And if I tried to leave for any length of time, she would fling hateful accusations at

me like I didn't care—that I was no more of a faith-
ful daughter than Big Mike had been as a husband.
For a while, I even had to take a hiatus from my job
because her doctor feared she would harm herself."

"Big Mike—is that your father?"

"Yes. His name is Michael, but since he was a
young boy, everyone has called him Big Mike."

"I see. I guess you must have been pretty angry
with Big Mike when all of this happened," he said,
while trying to imagine the hell that must have been
going on in Nicole's life.

"Well, I was somewhat angry," she agreed. "But
I've always loved Dad and I tried to look at things
with an open mind. He had reason to be unhappy.
His job kept him away from Fort Worth most of the
time, and Mom had become very uninterested in
anything going on with him, even when Big Mike
was home. They grew apart and his eye wandered—
I think it was that simple."

"If your mother was so dependent on you, how
did you manage to move out here? You mentioned
having a brother—did he take over caring for her?"

She groaned and closed her eyes. "No. Trace lives
in Louisiana and works on offshore drilling rigs.
I told him to stay there because there was hardly
any point to both of us disrupting our lives. And
anyway, Mom had plenty of money to hire private
nursing care or even a companion to make her feel

not so alone. But she refused. She wanted to cling to me instead."

"That must have been damned rough on you."

"Yes, especially when she would beg me not to leave her," Nicole agreed. "But you haven't heard the half of it yet. Less than a year after my parents divorced, Big Mike came back to Fort Worth and begged Angela to forgive him. And, of course, she did. Now they're remarried and happier than I've ever seen them. In fact, they're like two different people. Like newlyweds who can't keep their eyes or their hands off each other."

"Aw hell, you're kidding."

Her eyes opened to settle on his face. "I realize it sounds like some cheesy movie plot, but that's actually what happened. And once Mom was off the anxiety and depression meds, I decided it was time for me to break free. So here I am in Arizona living an entirely different life. Except that—"

"Except what? Surely you're thrilled that your parents got everything worked out."

"I am," she said. "And my father has told me more than once how grateful he was that I'd stuck through the rough times with Mom. But I—well, I should be ashamed of myself, Trey. Because I—still can't rid myself of the resentment I feel toward Mom, especially. That makes me sound awful and look even worse, doesn't it?"

He shook his head. "No. It seems pretty understandable to me. You didn't tell your father to go have an affair or divorce your mother. It wasn't your fault that when trouble hit, she was too emotionally weak to hold up."

She studied him for a moment before she sat up straight and covered her face with both hands. As Trey watched her, he feared she was going to cry, and he wasn't sure he'd know exactly how to console her. But then her hands fell away and she looked at him with a mixture of gratitude and misgiving.

"Thank you, for being so understanding. And I agree with you. It wasn't my fault that my parents' marriage crumbled. Nor was it my place to try to put it back to together. But, as children, we're supposed to take care of our parents when they're in need. After all, they took care of us until we became grown-ups, right?"

"Uh, mine tried. I'll put it that way," Trey admitted, while thinking of the years of struggling he and his mother had gone through because his father had moved on without them.

"I guess—it's just hard for me to forget all that I sacrificed to keep her from—well, for a long time I feared she might take her own life. She seemed that low in spirit. Then when Big Mike returned, Mom flipped a switch and was suddenly a different woman. That was hard to take. And now I feel like I've earned the right to live my own life the way I want to live it."

He reached for her hand and pressed it between his palms. "Are you saying your parents want something different for you?"

Her lips twisted to a wry slant. "Mom calls me every day, urging me to come back to Texas. There are some days I get three or four calls from her, along with a half-dozen text messages. Dad wants to buy me a new house, a car—whatever my heart desires just to get me to live near them. Sometimes, Trey, it gets to be almost more than I can bear."

Whatever her heart desires. Exactly what did Nicole's heart desire, he wondered. And where did he rate among the things she wanted in life? Did he want to be a part of her wishes?

Even as he attempted to answer the self-imposed question, that unexplained pressure returned to his chest. In an effort to ease the discomfort, he sat up and wrapped an arm around her shoulder.

"Sometimes it takes more than a thousand miles to fix a problem, Nicci. If you don't want to go back there, then it's up to you to make your feelings clear to your parents. No matter how much they might protest."

She let out a long sigh and then twisted her head just enough to give him a smile. "Roslyn is always telling me I need to get more of a spine. Sounds like you're giving me the same advice."

Deciding it was well past time to lighten the moment, Trey chuckled and, starting at her waist, climbed two fingers up the middle of her back. "Your backbone feels sturdy enough to me. All you need to do is use it."

He began easing her down on the bed and she let out a provocative chuckle. "What are you doing? Testing its flexibility?"

"I've decided it bends perfectly." Once she was settled on the mattress, his hands left her shoulders to cup around the backs of her thighs. "Now I think I need to examine your hamstrings. It would be awful if you pulled one. Everyone at the clinic would want to know why you're hobbling."

Chuckling under her breath, she pushed at his chest until he was lying flat on his back and her warm little body was draped over his.

"Maybe you should be the one worried about hobbling into work tomorrow."

She teased the words against the corner of his lips, and Trey wasn't surprised to feel a fresh surge of heat rush through his body.

His mouth curved into a taunting grin. "You're quite a woman," he said slyly. "First you starve me, now you threaten to cripple me. What next?"

Her gray eyes glittered as she gazed down at his face. "How about me making love to you?" she whispered.

Slipping his arms around her back, he pressed her tight against him and forgot everything except the warm, tender joy filling his heart.

"I'm all yours, sweet Nicci."

Chapter Nine

"Here you are!" Roslyn sang out as she practically skipped her way into the break room. "I went to the front desk and found Loretta sitting in for you."

Nicole pulled out the folding chair next to her and motioned for Roslyn to join her at the utility table.

"I kept waiting for a lull in the action, but it never came. Luckily, Loretta offered to take over so that I could eat my lunch."

Roslyn glanced at her watch. "Lunch! Nicci, it's two thirty in the afternoon. Why didn't you yell for help before now?"

Nicole shrugged. "No big deal. I wasn't that hungry anyway."

And why would she be? she thought wryly. The

enchilada meal that she and Trey had finally gotten around to eating at one thirty this morning had stuck with her until recently.

Roslyn sank into the adjoining chair and looked at her with kind concern. "I know you want to prove to Chandler and me and everyone else here at the clinic that you're a dedicated worker. But there's no need for you to go overboard. You're always here early and leaving late. You rarely take a short coffee break and—"

Nicole held up her hand to interrupt her friend's assessment. "Listen, I'm not trying to prove anything. I'm just doing my job. That's all."

Roslyn rolled her eyes, and as Nicole studied her pretty face, she realized the young woman who'd been her friend all those years back in Fort Worth was basically gone. Since Roslyn had moved here to Arizona, married Chandler and created a family, she'd morphed into a different person. Instead of being little more than Martin DuBose's sad, dutiful daughter, she was now a happy, confident wife and the mother of two children. She never stressed over the heavy workload at the clinic. Nor did she chew her fingernails if everything wasn't perfect at home; she took it all in stride.

"Well, I'm only trying to point out that you don't have to do your job quite so much."

"Don't worry. I'll pace myself." She returned the last section of her sandwich to its wrapper before she turned a thoughtful look at her friend. "Ros, when did you realize you were in love with Chandler?"

Roslyn's features twisted with comical confusion. "What is this? Are you doing some sort of survey on the subject of love?"

Hating the idea that she probably looked like a blushing teenager, Nicole grabbed her coffee cup and took a couple of sips. "I've been wondering, that's all."

Daring a peek at her friend, she watched Roslyn's brows form a straight line. No doubt she was worried about her, Nicole thought. She was acting out of the norm. But wasn't that typical behavior for a woman who'd fallen in love? To go around with her head in a foggy dream?

"Oh honey, don't tell me you're still agonizing over giving up Randy?" she said in a frustrated voice. "I remember how crushed you were when your dreams of marrying him ended. But face, it, when you told him you were staying in Texas with your mother instead of going with him to California, he didn't care enough to even put up a fight to win you over. A woman wants her man to love her passionately. To do everything humanly possible to keep her at his side. Randy was a sap. He wasn't the man for you."

"He went into the Marines, Ros. You can't say he lacked ambition or gumption." Even as Nicole said the words, she realized that Roslyn's assessment of the situation was right on target. Randy hadn't cared enough to fight for Nicole's love. In fact, he'd simply said he was disappointed with her decision not to marry him and walked away without a backward glance.

Roslyn snorted. "A guy with brawn and muscle can be a wimp in the ways that really count. And in my opinion Randy was a big one."

Nicole laughed with relief. "Thank God I didn't waste any more time on him."

Roslyn arched a brow at her. "I do believe you've seen the light."

Nicole smiled as the image of Trey's handsome face flickered into her mind's eye. "Seeing the truth changes everything. Now, back to my earlier question. How did you know it was love with Chandler?"

She tilted her blond head one way and then the other. "If you're looking for a simple answer, then I guess I realized I was in love with Chandler when I considered moving on to California. The idea of life without him was like staring into a black hole. It was incomprehensible."

Nicole sighed as her thoughts drifted back to last night and the intimacy she'd shared with Trey. Making love to him had changed everything for her. Now all her hopes and dreams and priorities led straight to him.

Roslyn's hand was suddenly waving in front of Nicole's line of vision.

"Yoo-hoo, Nicci? You're off in outer space!"

"Sorry. I was thinking about what you said," Nicole explained.

Leaning closer, Roslyn peered at her. "Why, Nicole Nelson, I believe there's a dreamy fog in your eyes! Have you—" Pausing, she left the table and went over to the open doorway. After a quick glance down the hallway, she shut the door, then returned to her chair and grabbed hold of Nicole's hands. "Have you fallen in love? With Trey?"

A hot blush stormed over Nicole's cheeks. "Go ahead and tell me I'm an idiot. For the past year or more, I've been avoiding men at every turn. I haven't wanted to think about marriage or love or anything remotely connected. My plan was to wait until—well, until I'd gathered some common sense together. I believed I needed to take the time to decide whether that's really what I wanted."

Roslyn laughed. "That's ridiculous! You don't have to ask yourself what you want! From the time we were young girls, all you ever talked about was being a wife and mother—having your own family. It's been your dream."

Nicole groaned ruefully. "Sure, I remember that dream. But it turned into a nightmare after going through my parents' divorce and remarriage fiasco. When I left Fort Worth, I had just about closed the door on wanting anything to do with love. But then I came out here and what do I do? Swoon over a man that I've only known for a few weeks! I must be out of my mind."

Roslyn shook her head. "Do you remember when I first started working here at the clinic? You thought I'd lost my mind. Me, city-girl Roslyn, helping nurse a bunch of sick animals. You thought I was mixed-up and probably making a mistake about leaving Fort Worth and my pampered life behind. I believe you even thought I was crazy for jumping into marriage with Chandler after I'd just given birth to another man's baby."

Deciding she had no option but to take the honest route, Nicole nodded. "Okay, I'll admit it, I'm guilty on all those counts. I can also see quite clearly that I was wrong about everything. You made all the right choices."

Roslyn's gave her an encouraging smile. "You'll make the right choices, too, dear Nicci. All you have to do is follow what your heart is telling you."

"I can do that. Trouble is, I don't really know what Trey is thinking or feeling about me. He, uh, likes me enough, I guess. But he's not one to talk much about his feelings or his wants for the future. The only plans he's mentioned is wanting land, cattle and horses. Nothing about a wife or children. And then he keeps giving me these impressions that he thinks I'm too good for him, or he's not good enough for me."

"Nicci, Trey needs time to adjust. You're a different type of woman than he's accustomed to dating."

Dating? Was that the word for it? The times she and Trey had spent together seemed like so much more. But maybe she was reading too much into his smiles and kisses, the tender way he touched and held her.

"What do you mean?" she asked. "Has Trey dated a lot? Loretta mentioned that he had a serious girlfriend once. But that's all."

Roslyn shook her head. "From what I know about Trey, his idea of dating is going to the Fandango to drink beer and dance with the local girls."

"I see," Nicole mumbled thoughtfully. "So it's not his nature to get serious over a woman?"

"I've never seen that side of him. But from what Chandler has told me, Trey had a couple of serious girlfriends in the past. Although, that was several years ago and long before I moved here and married Chandler. But as for you—I'm thinking Trey probably sees you as a princess sitting high up on a pedestal and he's a lowly court jester."

Nicole frowned at the thought. "That's plain silly. Just because my parents have money or that I've graduated from college doesn't make me a princess!"

"I understand that and so do you, but Trey needs time to figure it out for himself. That's what I think." Roslyn's gaze swept up to the clock on the wall, and she suddenly jumped to her feet. "Oh my gosh, I need to get back to the recovery room!"

Nicole began to gather the leftovers of her lunch. "Uh, Ros, I think I must've sidetracked you. Did you come in here hunting me for a reason?"

Roslyn snapped her fingers. "Right! I wanted to invite you to Chandler's birthday party Friday night at Three Rivers Ranch. Maureen's shindigs are always fun, so I think you'll enjoy it. And Trey will be there, too, so you shouldn't get lonely."

She winked at Nicole, then hurried out of the breakroom.

A half hour past the clinic's regular closing time, Trey and Chandler had left the treatment barn and were on their way to the clinic building when Nicole met them halfway on the beaten path.

Since Trey had left her house in the wee hours of this morning, he'd been so busy he'd not had the opportunity to see her or even send a text. Now as his gaze took in her wrapped red dress sprinkled with yellow flowers and the long hair draped upon her shoulders, Trey felt his heart jump into a happy jig. Has this woman really held him close and rained passionate kisses, not only on his lips, but on every other part of his body? Had she really made love to him as though he was the most desirable, precious thing she'd ever touched? He was still having trouble believing the night had been real instead of a fantastic dream.

Chandler was the first to speak. "Hey, Nicci, you should be headed home, shouldn't you?"

She shook her head. "Not yet," she answered. "I needed to let you know there's an emergency call on the phone. A horse has been injured at a roping arena south of town. I've put the person on hold—in case you need to speak with her."

"Thanks. I'll take the call in my office," he said to Nicole. To Trey he added, "I'll need to get some meds from the supply room. You might make sure the truck has all our equipment."

"Right. I'll wait for you there," Trey told him.

As Chandler hurried away, Trey turned his attention to Nicci. The soft smile on her face had him wishing he could gather her up and kiss her right here in the open, no matter who might be watching.

"Hi," she said gently.

"Hi, yourself. I've tried all day to find a moment to text you, but it never came. We've been swamped."

She moved closer and placed her hand on his forearm. "I know. And it looks like you're far from finished. I guess this means you won't make it by the house tonight."

There was a shade of disappointment in her voice, but not the petulant kind. The idea that she could be so understanding made him want her even more.

"Wrong. I'll be there. Even if it's midnight and I have to wake you."

Her chuckle was incredibly sexy, and Trey couldn't stop himself from bending and placing a quick kiss on her forehead.

"You won't have to wake me," she promised, then gave him a little push toward Chandler's work truck parked beneath a mesquite tree. "Now you'd better go before Doc finds you dawdling with the receptionist."

Close to three hours later, Chandler and Trey were standing outside one of the clinic's horse stalls watching a palomino gelding limp over to a water trough.

Once the two men had arrived on the scene and Chandler had carefully examined the horse, they'd managed to load the animal into a trailer and transport it here to the clinic. Since then, they'd made several X-rays of the horse's foot and cannon bone and determined there were no life-ending breaks, only a strained tendon.

After treating the horse with injections and a leg soaking, the worried owner had finally decided it was safe for her to go home and leave her beloved animal in Chandler's care for the next few days.

"At least he's going to get well," Trey said.

"Yes. Luck was with him. Anytime a horse collides with a steer and both animals are running full blast, the result usually isn't pretty." He slapped a hand on Trey's shoulder. "Let's go home. What do you say?"

Trey wasn't going home. Not in the technical sense. But he was beginning to think of home as anywhere he was with Nicole, and that was a scary thought. One he'd been trying to ward off ever since he'd climbed out of her bed and drove to his place.

"Will Ranger be all right, you think?" Trey asked, as the two men turned away from the penned horse and started toward the parking area. "I can drive back over in a few hours and check on him."

"No need for that. The pain meds will last until tomorrow evening and hopefully the steroids will keep the swelling down. All he needs now is rest. And speaking of rest, you look like you could use some yourself. Did you eat lunch?"

"Don't worry about me, Doc. I'm fine." The mere idea of being with Nicole again was enough to make him feel like he could jump a dozen fences, forward and backward.

"I don't have to tell you we've been as busy as hell around here. But we've been this swamped with work before and it never made you look like this. Have you been sleeping?"

Damn, did he look that wrung out? "Uh—yeah. I've been catching a few winks here and there. Only last night Nicci had me over for dinner and I stayed kinda late," he said, while thinking that was the most he was going to admit to Chandler.

"Uh-huh. I'm beginning to understand now," Chandler said slyly. "Are you two getting close?"

If they'd gotten any closer, it might've killed him, Trey thought. "Guess you could call it that. We— enjoy each other's company. For now, that is."

Chandler paused his long stride to peer at Trey through the falling twilight. "For now? What the hell does that mean?"

Trey wished Chandler wouldn't push him for an explanation. He was already having enough trouble trying not to think too far ahead. It was easier on his mind and his heart to stay in the present and not dwell on the time when this thing with Nicole came to end. And it would. Because sooner or later she'd wake up from her dreamworld and see that he didn't fit into her future plans.

Shrugging, Trey tried to sound casual, but his troubled thoughts brought a tinge of bitterness to his voice. "We've had this discussion before. You know nothing lasts with me."

Chandler's brows slowly arched upward as he studied Trey's face. "Have you stopped to think that Nicci might be expecting more from you? Maybe you ought to make it clear to her that you're not a serious kind of guy. You'd be doing her, and your-self, a favor."

It took lots of pushing and prodding to stir Trey's

temper. Especially from Chandler. The man was his best friend in the world. But at this moment, curse words were boiling on the tip of Trey's tongue.

"Nicci is a grown woman. She understands where I'm coming from," he said sharply. "And I know where I stand with her. So there's no need for you to worry about either of us!"

If Chandler was surprised by Trey's retort, he didn't show it. Instead, he laughed. A fact that irked Trey even more.

"Me worry about my best buddy? Why would I do that? Apparently, you have everything under control and exactly the way you want it." He lifted a hand in farewell. "See you tomorrow, Trey."

By the time Chandler opened the truck door to climb behind the wheel, a feeling of remorse washed over Trey and he hurried over to him.

"Doc, wait a minute."

With one boot resting on the running board, Chandler paused to look over his shoulder. "You wanted to say something else?"

Trey cleared his throat, then wiped a hand over his face. "I'm being a jackass. Go ahead and tell me so. I deserve it."

Chandler laughed again. "If you ask me, you're putting yourself in a mighty high animal bracket," he joked.

Grinning sheepishly, he said, "You're right. Donkeys aren't dumb, just stubborn. Sort of like me—sometimes."

"Sometimes?"

Trey chuckled. "Yeah. Sorry, I guess I'm tired and a little on edge."

Stepping back to the ground, Chandler asked, "Why? You worried about this thing you've started with Nicci?"

Trey let out a heavy breath. "I don't understand it. I've never been happier in my life. Nicci is—she's just wonderful. But deep down I know that sooner rather than later I'm going to disappoint her."

Chandler shook his head. "All you have to do is be yourself and be honest with her. I promise you won't disappoint her."

Sighing, Trey looked down at the ground. "That's not exactly what I mean."

"Hell!"

The curse word jerked Trey's gaze up to Chandler's face. "What's the—"

"Trey, sometimes you're slower than molasses! And sometimes, like right at this moment, I'd like to set the seat of your jeans on fire!"

Trey lifted his arms and let them flop against his sides in a helpless gesture. "See? If I make you so frustrated, just think—"

"Close your trap and listen!" Chandler interrupted. "Nicci doesn't want a rich man. Nor does she want a perfect man."

"How do you know that?"

Chandler groaned with frustration. "I'm a genius. That's how! Now get the hell out of here before I kick your rear!"

"Mom, I really think you and Dad should take a vacation. A long one. Some place that's new and interesting to both of you," Nicole suggested as she stood at the kitchen counter, attempting to make cold-cut sandwiches with one hand while the other held the cell phone to her ear.

"That sounds great, Nicci dear, but Big Mike has to fly to New Mexico and oversee a job out there for the next month," Angela said. "That means I'll have to find something here to keep myself occupied."

The whiny sound to her mother's voice sent an uneasy thought darting through Nicole's mind. Was her parents' relationship already headed on a downward spiral again?

"Why don't you go to New Mexico with Dad," Nicole suggested. "I'm sure he'd love your company. And you wouldn't have to be home alone and wondering what to do with all the time on your hands."

"I wouldn't be alone if you were living back in the city," she pointed out. "Oh, Nicci, we used to have such fun going shopping together, having lunch and gossiping about all our friends. It could be that way again, honey."

Nicole closed her eyes and pinched the bridge of

her nose as she recalled the time when she and her mother had been very close. Those happy years were something Nicole would always cherish. But neither of them could go back to those days. They were over. Just like Nicole's life in Fort Worth was over.

You have to quit worrying about your parents and think about your own future. You've taken the first step by moving out here and away from them. Now get a backbone and make the most of it.

With Roslyn's advice suddenly echoing through her thoughts, Nicole straightened her shoulders and spoke firmly, "Not on a permanent basis, Mom. I'll come back for short visits. But that's all. You have to accept my decision. You're fine now. Both mentally and physically, you don't need me to lean on. You have to accept the fact that I can't be around to fill in for Dad's absence."

She could hear Angela's soft gasp and knew her mother had been shocked by her daughter's frankness. But back when Angela had been under a doctor's supervision, he'd told Nicole that the best thing she could do for her mother was to force her to stand on her on two feet. For everyone's sake, Nicole had to hold fast to the doctor's advice.

"I don't want you to fill in for him. I—"

"Yes, you do!" Nicole interrupted before her mother could continue to lie to herself. "And you have to stop it, Mom. Dad needs you."

"Big Mike has his job. He's always had his job,"

Angela argued, then added in a placating tone, "But don't worry about your parents, darling. We're better than ever—the happiest we've been in years."

"And I want you two to stay happy. You need to focus on Dad instead of trying to lure me back to Texas. If you really care about his feelings, then you won't mind bearing up to a little desert dust and making yourself comfortable in portable housing. He would love having your company and I know it would be good for you to be there with him."

"Are you serious? What would I do?"

Nicole refrained from rolling her eyes. After all, it wasn't totally her mother's fault that she'd become so spoiled over the years. Big Mike had done a good job of pampering her. So much so that Angela considered her own needs rather than those of the people she supposedly loved.

"You could start by taking care of Dad's needs and showing him how much you appreciate all the hard work he's put in over the years to give you anything and everything you've ever wanted. Including two children."

A long stretch of silence told Nicole that, for once, she'd managed to grab her mother's attention.

Finally, Angela said, "Why, Nicci, what have they done to you out there? I've never heard you talk like this. And anyway, I thought you were still angry with your father for his—well, bad behavior."

The last thread of Nicole's patience very nearly

snapped. "I'm still angry with the both of you," she said bluntly. "And I need time and space to get over it. So please give me that much."

"Space?" Angela croaked. "You've already put a thousand miles between us. Isn't that enough space?"

Nicole realized she'd be wasting her time trying to explain the context of space to her mother. Angela was focused on one thing. Getting her life back as it used to be before her marriage dissolved, before Nicole decided she deserved to have her own life.

"Sorry, Mom. I've got to get off the phone. I have a date and he'll be arriving any minute."

Angela gasped. "A date! But what about Randy?"

Biting back the urge to scream, she gave her mother a curt goodbye and ended the call.

Fifteen minutes later, Nicole had pushed her mother's annoying call out of her head and had just finished making a pitcher of ice tea to go with the sandwiches when she heard Trey's knock.

Her heart humming with joy, she hurried to the foyer and opened the door to find him standing hat in hand, smiling back at her. Nicole didn't waste time with words. She reached for his hand and tugged him over the threshold and into her arms.

Hugging her tight, he said, "Mmm! If I'd known I was going to get this kind of reception, I would've driven faster."

The scent she'd come to know as uniquely his wrapped around her senses as she buried her face in the middle of his chest. "I've been thinking about you all day and wanting to do this."

He said, "I hope you've been thinking about this, too."

He tilted her face up to his, and the long, searching kiss he planted on her lips left her sighing for more. "You almost make me want to forget about eating," she admitted.

A sexy lopsided grin carved out dimples in both his cheeks. "Almost?"

Chuckling under her breath, she stepped around him and dealt with closing and locking the door. "We're not going to get sidetracked tonight. Not when I've gone to the trouble of making a stack of sandwiches with my own two little hands."

"Just for me? I feel honored," he teased.

She laughed again, and as she clasped her hand around his, she realized that Trey was the only man who'd ever made her feel truly deep-down happy inside. It was like he'd unlocked a secret part of her that was filled with nothing but joy.

"One of these days I might actually learn how to cook something edible. And then I'll fix you a real dinner," she promised.

"What's more real than a sandwich?"

Laughing, she led him out of the living room and into the intersecting hallway. "You know where the bathroom is. This time I'll wait for you in the kitchen."

As he headed down the hallway, he taunted playfully over his shoulder, "Fraidy cat."

Inside the kitchen, Nicole put the platter of sandwiches, along with a basket of chips, onto the table and was filling two iced glasses with tea when Trey emerged through the swinging doors.

As he drew closer, she could see he'd washed the dust from his face and combed damp fingers through his blond hair. The sleeves of his white cotton shirt were rolled back upon his tanned forearms, while the tail was tucked neatly into the waistband of his jeans. He looked incredibly rugged and sexy, and as her gaze drank in his tempting image, she wondered if she'd gone crazy. Eating a sandwich was hardly the first thing on her wish list tonight.

He said, "You look like you're about to laugh. Do I look funny or something?"

Her cheeks warm, she walked over to the table where he was standing behind one of the wooden chairs.

"Actually, I was thinking I didn't want you to get the idea that I only wanted you for sex."

His brows shot straight up. "No wonder you were about to laugh. That idea is hilarious. Where did you come up with it, anyway?"

He pulled out a chair and helped her into it. After she was settled comfortably in the seat, she said in a teasing voice, "Well, I haven't exactly behaved in a

shy manner around you. You're going to start thinking I'm a brazen hussy."

Chuckling, he joined her in the chair sitting kitty-
corner to her left elbow. "I'd rather think I'm so irresistible that you can't control yourself," he teased.

And he'd be right, Nicole thought. She was drawn
to him in so many ways that she couldn't resist.

"I am glad you didn't have to work very late tonight." She pushed the platter of sandwiches toward
his plate. "How did things go with the injured horse?"

"Good. We brought him back to the clinic and
Doc will be treating him for the next few days. It's
going to take a long recuperation, but eventually he'll
be fine."

"I'm happy to hear that," she said, then casting
him a curious glance, she abruptly changed the subject. "Did Roslyn talk to you about Chandler's birthday party? They're having it at Three Rivers. I forgot
to ask if the party is supposed to be a surprise, so
I wasn't sure if Chandler might have already mentioned it to you."

Nodding, he speared a pair of sandwich halves
onto his plate. "Maureen always puts on such big
shindigs that it would be impossible to make it a surprise. Doc has already invited me. I promised him
I'd be there. What about you?"

"I assured Ros I'd be there," she said, then slanted
him a hopeful glance. "I thought the two of us might
go together. It's a long drive out there."

"Sure. I'd like that," he said.

She lifted a sandwich to her lips but lowered it back to her plate before she could take a bite. "Sorry, Trey," she said sheepishly. "I'm being forward—again—putting the two of us together without considering the thought that you might want to go alone. Just tell me if you'd rather go stag. I won't mind."

He shook his head. "I'm here because I want to spend time with you. As much time as I can before—"

He broke off so suddenly that her expression turned quizzical. "Before what?"

Clearing his throat, he said, "Nothing. Er—I only started to say before Doc and I get even busier. That's all."

Skeptical now, she frowned at him. "I can't imagine you two being busier. You're always running all over Yavapai County and parts of Maricopa County, too. If you got any busier, you'd be working twenty hours of the day."

"That's actually happened before."

Her lips twisted to a wry slant. "Somehow that doesn't surprise me."

She picked up her sandwich and managed to take one bite before a cell phone lying on the cabinet counter dinged to announce an incoming message.

Trey glanced in the direction of the sound. "I hear your phone. Were you expecting anything important?"

"No. I'm certain it's my mother. We had a conversation not long before you arrived. Now she thinks I'm angry with her."

"Are you?"

"Not exactly angry. More like frustrated. And a bit worried."

The weary sound in her voice sent a ripple of unease through Trey. What would he do if she suddenly announced she had to move back to Fort Worth to deal with her mother?

You've been left behind before, Trey. Your ego was squashed for a while, but you got over it.

Yeah, but things were different this time, Trey argued with the daunting voice in his head. The feelings he had for Nicole were already rooted deep inside him. Tearing them out would leave him full of empty holes.

Trying not to think about that possibility, he asked, "Is something wrong with her?"

"Nothing new. Dad has to leave soon on a work trip to New Mexico. Instead of going with him, Mom thinks I should be there to fill the void." Shaking her head, she said, "It's so wrong, Trey."

"I thought you told me their marriage was going great now. Are you worried that might be changing?"

Nodding, she said, "The way I see it, marriages take work, and I'm not sure Mom has that much work ethic."

She'd barely gotten the words out when the phone dinged twice in rapid succession. Nicole put down her sandwich. "Excuse me. I'm going to take care of this."

Trey watched her walk over to the cabinet, and after a quick glance at the screen, she punched a button on the side of the cell phone, then dropped it into a drawer and pushed it shut.

Out of earshot and out of sight, Trey thought. But was that enough to push the problem out of her mind, at least for tonight? She'd explained what had happened to her parents and how she'd felt the need to get away and move here to Arizona. But with her mother continuing to tug at her, how much longer could she stand being torn between her life here in Wickenburg and her family back in Texas?

"Sorry for the interruption," she said as she rejoined him at the table.

He made himself smile at her. "Don't worry about it."

She reached over and placed a hand on his forearm. Her gentle touch reminded him how much he needed her, how much it meant to him to be a part of her life. But he was very afraid to let himself love again or dream of having a family. He'd tried in the past and failed and it had taken him years to get over the hurt and humiliation of being rejected, not once, but twice. He couldn't bear to think of falling short in Nicole's eyes—of losing her.

"Trey," she said softly, "this is our time—for me and you only."

He gave her a pointed glance. "If an emergency happened right now, Doc would call and I'd have to go help him. That would be a huge interruption."

"A call from Chandler would be different. That would be a medical crisis. Mom isn't in crisis. She's in denial."

"You sound certain of that."

"I am. And I'm very certain that I want you here with me."

As Trey's gaze scanned the gentle expression on her face, he realized Chandler had given him sound advice when he'd suggested he be himself and be honest. Being himself would be easy enough, he decided. But how could he be honest and admit that he didn't want to live without her?

Even if he had all kinds of courage, he couldn't admit such a thing to her. She'd think he'd gone and fallen in love with her. And that wouldn't be true. Trey had quit falling in love a long, long time ago.

"Trey, are you okay?"

Her voice jerked him out of his reverie and he saw that she was leaning toward him, a look of real concern on her face.

Thinking he probably looked like a fish lying on a creek bank, he snapped his mouth shut and swallowed hard. "I, uh, was just thinking."

"Must have been some deep thinking," she remarked.

He laughed in an effort to cover up his embarrassment. "No. Just thinking about the birthday party and—other things. And there's something I've been thinking about asking you."

Her face lit up with a smile. "If I'm ready to go panning again? I've been thinking we need to go again—and soon. It would be nice to put a few more nuggets into your ranch kitty."

"That would be nice. But there's somewhere I thought—" He reached for her soft little hand and squeezed it. "Uh—how would you like to drive over to Aguila and meet Granny?"

Her jaw dropped as she stared wide-eyed at him. "Seriously? You really want me to meet your grand-mother?"

She made it sound like meeting his grandmother was the next thing to a marriage proposal. Trey was wondering if he'd made a mistake by offering the in-vitation when she suddenly hopped out of her chair and wrapped her arms around his neck. But as soon as she began to rain kisses all over his face, he real-ized that anything that made her happy made him happy, too.

Laughing between the smacks she was placing on his cheeks and chin, he said, "Sure, I want you to meet her, or I wouldn't have asked."

"Oh, I can't wait! When can we go? Tomorrow night?"

Her eagerness amazed him. It also made him feel about ten feet tall. Was that what a woman's love did for a man? he wondered. Made him believe he could lift the whole world and balance it in one hand?

Hey, Trey, you're getting way ahead of yourself. You might have Nicole's attention, but she's never talked about loving you. She's never hinted at the word.

Refusing to listen to the doubting voice going through his head, Trey said, "Granny works late at the café on Thursday and Friday nights. And we'll be at Doc's party on Saturday. I'll see if she's going to be home Sunday. Can you go then?"

Pulling her head back, she touched the tip of her nose to his. "I'll be ready and waiting!"

With a hand at the back of her head, he pulled her face near enough to fasten his lips over hers. She moaned softly, and without breaking the kiss, she slowly sank into his lap.

When she wrapped her arms around his neck, Trey gathered her closer and deepened the kiss until their tongues were mating and his hand was sliding over her hip and onto her buttocks. Along the way, desire began to lick at the edges of his brain and send red-hot signals to the rest of his body.

He kissed her until he could no longer breathe and was forced to pull his mouth away from the intoxicating sweetness of her lips.

"We haven't finished eating," he murmured huskily.

Her gray eyes were like silver smoke as her lips tilted into a sexy smile. "Who cares about eating?"

He chuckled under his breath. "You said we weren't going to get sidetracked. Remember?"

"I have a very short memory." Smiling impishly, she tugged him up from the chair.

Trey willingly allowed her to lead him out of the kitchen, and as they walked hand in hand down the hallway to her bedroom, he realized he'd been all wrong when he'd called himself a stubborn jackass. No, this thing he had with Nicole had turned him into a helpless little lamb, too lost in her charms to stop her from shepherding him straight off a cliff.

Chapter Ten

Saturday turned out to be a blazing hot day, but as darkness fell over Three Rivers Ranch house, the temperature dropped dramatically. To make it more comfortable for the birthday party guests, a fire had been built in a large stone firepit located at one end of the covered patio. Festive colored lights hung from the rafters, while a portable bar had been set up to provide before-dinner cocktails.

With her back to the warmth of the flames, Nicole's gaze vacillated from the family and friends milling about on the patio to the ranch yard in the far distance. A half hour ago, Chandler and his younger brother Holt had insisted Trey join them on a trip to the horse barn to check on a very pregnant mare. So far none of the three men had returned to the party.

Nicole was wondering if a medical emergency had detained them when she spotted Holt's wife, Isabelle, walking toward her. Dressed in a floral skirt and blouse, the lovely blonde was carrying a long-stemmed glass filled with orange-colored liquid and slices of citrus fruit.

Having met her several weeks ago, Nicole already regarded the woman as a friend. Besides being warm and down-to-earth, she'd also learned Isabelle was an excellent horse woman, and along with being a wife and mother, she worked her own horse ranch, the Blue Stallion.

"Nicci, where's your drink? You need to get in the partying mood," she scolded playfully.

Nicole smiled. "I just finished a margarita. If I had another, I'd have to be helped to the dinner table."

Laughing lightly, Isabelle turned her back to the heat radiating from the fire. "Same here. This will be my one and only cocktail. And speaking of the dinner table, Maureen has decided to have dinner inside tonight. Even with the fire, our food would be cold by the time we filled our plates."

"It is a bit chilly." She glanced over at Isabelle. The woman didn't appear a bit fidgety about Holt's absence. No doubt she was probably accustomed to her husband disappearing in the middle of a dinner party. "Did you bring your baby with you tonight? I've not had a chance to see him yet."

Smiling fondly, Isabelle nodded. "Carter is upstairs with the rest of his little cousins. Probably trying to hoard up all the little horses he can find in the toy box. For some reason, he's obsessed with the animals," she added with an impish wink.

"I don't suppose both his parents being horse trainers has anything to do with that," Nicole joked.

"Not a thing," Isabelle said with a chuckle. And in case you're wondering, Roslyn is still upstairs trying to get Billy to sleep. If you'd like, we'll go up later on and you can see the whole brood of kids."

"I'd like that," Nicole told her. "I've been trying to remember all the children's names. I know Evelyn and Billy belong to Roslyn and Chandler but I'm not sure about the rest. There're so many I get them mixed up."

Isabelle smiled. "Maureen calls her grandchildren the little herd. By the way, what do you think of my mother-in-law?"

The first time Nicole had visited Three Rivers to meet Roslyn's family, Maureen had walked into the room wearing jeans and boots and a crumpled cowboy hat with a stampede string drawn tight beneath her chin. Nicole had been amazed by the woman.

"Oh my, she's everything and more than I expected. She's so beautiful and warm. She seems ageless."

Isabelle nodded. "Not to mention strong, hardworking and loving. There's no way any of her daughters-in-law could ever fill her shoes. Blake, Chandler's older brother, manages this ranch and does a fine job of it, but underneath, their mother, Maureen, keeps the wheels turning."

"Speaking of beautiful women, your mother is no slouch," Nicole said of Gabby Leman, a lovely blonde, who'd been hanging on to her husband's arm ever since the couple strolled out here to the patio. "And her husband, Sam, is just delightful. It's amazing that he's in his seventies and able to work as foreman of the Bar X."

Loving pride shone on Isabelle's face, and Nicole had to wonder how it would feel to have a mother she could count on to be strong and understanding. Back in Texas those who knew Angela would say that wealth had spoiled her. But after being around the Hollisters, Nicole wasn't so sure. Maureen had been blessed with incredible wealth, yet she appeared to be a pillar for her family. Gabby was a successful artist, but she was happy to live a down-to-earth life with her cowboy.

Isabelle replied, "Lots of people predicted their marriage would never work. And not just because Sam is more than twenty years older than Mother. The fact that she's an artist and originally from San Diego and he's a rawhide-tough cowboy makes it look like such a mismatch. But none of that matters to them. They adore each other."

Nicole felt the same way about herself and Trey. They were different, too, and yet when they were together, it was like everything fit perfectly.

"They're lucky," Nicole said, "to have found each other and to be so happy and in love."

"So true. I was divorced when I met Holt. Back then I wasn't necessarily looking for love. Funny how it seems to find a person even when you're trying to avoid it." She sipped her drink, then turned a clever smile on Nicole. "Roslyn tells me you and Trey came to the party together tonight."

Nicole's cheeks grew warm. "We did. He's gone with Chandler and Holt to the horse barn right now."

Isabelle laughed. "And that was a half hour ago. Holt loses track of time when he's with his horses. And a mare that's foaling is a real party for those guys."

"Taking care of animals makes Trey happy," Nicole told her. "And that's good, because I want him to be happy."

Isabelle regarded her closely. "You sound like a woman who really cares about her guy."

Her guy. Nicole wanted to think of Trey as being her man. That the feelings between them were growing into an unbreakable bond. But so far, she was still waiting for him to give her a sign that their relationship meant more to him than physical pleasure.

"We've not known each other all that long," Nicole replied.

"Time is irrelevant," she said with a clever grin. "The first minute I saw Holt, I felt like an earthquake had hit me. And back then he was such a womanizer that I tried to convince myself that I despised him. Obviously, my strategy failed."

Nicole was thinking how loopy she'd felt when she'd first laid eyes on Trey when Isabelle suddenly gestured to the far end of the patio.

"Speaking of men, here they come," Isabelle said. "And if we're lucky, the mare will hold off until we eat dinner."

Through the years, Trey had attended many Hollister parties. Some had been huge affairs, others low-key. But he'd never had a date at his side. Especially one like Nicole. Now as the group headed into the house for dinner, he gave her a rueful smile.

"Sorry we were gone so long to the barn, Nicci."

"No problem," she replied. "Isabelle has been keeping me company. How was the mare?"

"Doc thinks she'll deliver in the next few hours. Two of Holt's assistants are keeping an eye on her right now."

She looked incredibly lovely tonight in a green-and-white strapless dress with a white lace shawl draped around her creamy shoulders. Her hair swung like a bright flame against her back and reminded Trey of the times he'd tangled his fingers in the silky strands and fastened his mouth over hers.

He was quickly becoming obsessed with her, he decided, and the fact was starting to worry him. But how did a man go about turning off the feelings in his heart?

"Chandler is probably hoping she'll hold off until tomorrow."

Her remark interrupted his thoughts, and he managed to chuckle. "Are you kidding? Doc thinks it's fun when a mare foals on his birthday. Just like there hasn't already been thirty or forty foals here on Three Rivers born on this day. Some are even named after him. Like Doc Do Too Much, CH Star and Chandler's Charge. He loves his job."

"Yes, and I think you love your job, too," she said with a knowing smile.

He slanted her a guilty look. "Just a little."

Inside the house, Trey and Nicole followed the crowd into a long dining room where three separate tables were set up to accommodate the large number of guests.

Nicole was seated to Trey's right side, while Taggart O'Brien was to his left. Beyond the Three Rivers Ranch foreman was his wife, Emily-Ann, who'd recently given birth to a boy they'd named Brody. Across the table, Holt and Isabelle were gazing at each other as though they were the only two people in the room.

Each of the Hollisters had a loving mate, he thought. Even Maureen had moved past the tragedy of losing her husband, Joel, and now seemed to be head over heels in love with his brother, Gil Hollister.

As Trey looked around at all the happy couples in the room, he couldn't help but feel like a little lost doggy. Everybody had somebody, he thought. Not just for tonight, but forever.

Why the hell are you feeling sorry for yourself, Trey? You have a beautiful woman sitting next to you, and she looks at you with stars in her eyes. If you really wanted a lasting family like the Hollisters, you'd be telling Nicci how much you loved her. How much you wanted the two of you to spend the rest of your lives together. Instead, you get scared if you even think she's going to mention the word love. You're a coward. Nothing but a sniveling coward.

"Trey, are you coming down with something?" Holt asked. "You look like you've eaten too many green apples. Is Nicci making you sick?"

A spate of chuckles penetrated Trey's wandering thoughts, and he glanced blankly around the table before his gaze settled on Holt's teasing face. "Did you say something to me?"

"I said you look miserable. I realize this isn't like going to the Fandango, but Mom does throw a decent party."

Hoping his face wasn't red, Trey said, "Oh—it's a great party." He glanced over at Nicole's curious expression, then back to Holt. "I was doing some thinking. And Doc always did say it made me sick to use my brain," he attempted to joke.

"Want to share those deep thoughts of yours?" Nicole asked.

The impish little smile on her face made him want to grab her and kiss her and forget all about the doubts rattling around in his head.

Snatching at the first thing that came to his mind, he said, "I—uh—was just noticing how especially happy Maureen looks tonight."

The thought was partly true, Trey decided. Earlier, when they'd first entered the dining room, he'd noticed the Hollister matriarch standing next to Gil, holding his hand and smiling up at him in the same endearing way that Nicole smiled at him.

"Maureen is happy," Isabelle spoke up. "Gil has changed her life for the better."

"Mom's hopes are high right now," Holt said, then added in a lower voice, "Joe and the Phoenix police are planning a meeting with Ginny Patterson. Sometime in the next few days. Mom believes the woman can fill in the blank spots about Dad's death."

"And that's the only thing that's holding Maureen back from actually planning a wedding with Gil," Isabelle added.

Next to Trey, Taggart quickly added, "I can tell you that Blake has his hopes up, too. We all do."

"Yes," Holt agreed with the ranch foreman. "For years we've had a cloud hanging over us, and we're praying that Ginny Patterson is finally going to help shine some light."

Trey started to question Holt about what this so-called meeting with the woman was going to involve, but the food suddenly arrived and everyone turned their attention to eating.

For the remainder of the party, the subject of Joel's death and the hope to solve it wasn't mentioned again, until much later when Trey and Nicole were driving back to Wickenburg.

"The whole thing is so—well, just thinking about it makes me shiver," Nicole said. "Who knows if this Ginny woman can be trusted? She might lead Joe and Connor into a trap?"

"We don't know if Joe and Connor will actually be in on the meeting or if the Phoenix police will handle the whole thing. Either way, they're professionals. They'll know how to deal with the situation."

She pondered his words for a moment before she finally said, "Yes, I suppose so. I wonder if Chandler and Roslyn know about this plan. Has he mentioned anything to you about it?"

"Yes, they know. The whole family has been waiting anxiously for Ginny Patterson to finally agree to a definite date for the meeting. Now it looks like that's finally in the process of getting done. I only hope it gives them answers." He looked over to see her head resting against the back of the seat, her eyelids lowered to sleepy slits. Just looking at her made his heart ache with feelings so strange and strong that he could never begin to understand them. "Have I told you how gorgeous you look tonight?"

A faint smile touched her lips. "Maybe two or three times. And you're changing the subject."

"You *are* my subject."

"Is that why you've been so distracted tonight?" she asked. "Even when we were dancing, I had the feeling you were somewhere else."

To add to the festivities, Maureen had hired a small three-piece band and pushed aside the living room furniture to make space for dancing. Trey had hoped having Nicole in his arms and moving to the music would help soothe the uneasiness that had come over him during the evening. Instead, it had made him even more impatient to get her alone.

"I was somewhere else," he admitted. "I was in bed making love to you."

She leaned across the console and reached for his hand. "We're almost home, darling."

Home. Yes, something about tonight had changed Trey's definition of that word. To have a real home, it took two people loving each other, working together, laughing at the good times and crying through the bad. It meant making roots together. And that meant he had to believe Nicole would never want to go back to Texas. He had to put his trust in her and truly believe she was different than the women who'd hurt him in the past.

Hours later, Nicole lay curled against Trey's warm body, her head pillowed on his arm as she gazed past the open curtain of the bedroom window. A moment ago, she'd heard the distant sound of a rooster crowing, and even though she couldn't see the clock on the nightstand, she knew that daylight would soon be pushing away the moonlight.

The party at Three Rivers had lasted for hours, and Nicole had enjoyed it immensely. Still, she'd been relieved when Trey had finally suggested they leave. He'd not been himself tonight. Even while they'd made love, she'd felt a part of him was far away.

She'd hoped that sleep would blot out her nagging thoughts. But instead of sleeping, she'd lain wide-awake, listening to Trey's even breathing and wondering what was in his heart. Why couldn't he share his feelings with her?

Maybe because his feelings for you aren't worth sharing, Nicole. Did you ever think of that? Just because he's in your bed doesn't mean he loves you, or anything close to it. You're dreaming. Hoping for something that is never going to be.

The mocking voice going on in her head caused tears to fill her eyes, and she prayed the salty moisture wouldn't roll down her cheek and onto his arm. Not for anything did she want him to wake and find her crying.

"You should be asleep."

The unexpected sound of his voice caused her to rapidly blink her watery eyes and attempt to swallow away the lump in her throat.

"You should be, too," she murmured. "We're going to be red-eyed when we go to see your grandmother later today. Do you still want to go?"

His cheek rubbed against the top of her head. "Sure. Why wouldn't I?"

"I thought—you might be out of the mood."

His hand slid gently down her arm to rest on the curve of her hip. "I want us to go. I don't know why you're thinking my mood is off."

With her back still to him, she drew in a deep breath and closed her eyes. "I'm sorry, Trey. I guess I'm just being a woman and getting the feeling that—" Turning to face him, she rested a hand in the middle of his chest. "Maybe you're getting tired of me."

"Tired?" His laugh was incredulous. "That's not going to happen."

The moonlight slanting through the windows illuminated his face. She carefully studied each rugged feature before she finally asked, "Do you remember after we went to the Wagon Wheel and I asked you what you would do if a woman got serious about you? You said you'd probably run. You've never explained why. Did a woman hurt you?"

He was silent for so long that Nicole had given

up on an answer, but then he sighed and turned his gaze toward the ceiling.

"I really don't want to talk about it, Nicci."

Rejection washed over her, and she quickly sat up and swung her legs over the edge of the mattress. "Oh. Okay."

His hand was suddenly wrapping around the side of her waist. "Where are you going?"

"To the kitchen. To make coffee." Anything would be better than lying next to him and thinking about things that made her want to burst into tears.

"You're angry with me," he stated.

"No. Just disappointed. That's all."

Suddenly he was sitting behind her and his hands were on her shoulders, drawing her back against his warn chest. "Doc told me that if I was honest with you, then you'd never be disappointed in me. I guess maybe I'd better be honest with you now."

Frowning, she twisted her head around to look at him. "I don't want you to do or say anything just because you feel I'm pressuring you. That's not good. So let's forget this. Okay?"

She started to rise, but he held her fast.

"It's not okay. I should've told you in the beginning that I—well, let's just say I tried the serious thing a couple of times before. Both of them ended in a bad way. For me, that is. Not for the women."

After Loretta and Roslyn had hinted about his past romances, she'd been thinking it would help her to understand him better if she knew what had happened. But now, the deepest part of her was revolting against the image of him loving another woman.

Trying to brace herself, she asked, "Serious? Like considering marriage?"

He nodded. "I was only twenty-one back then. Rhonda worked as a farrier's assistant. I thought we'd make a perfect match and so did she. Until she got the chance for a high-paying job on a ranch near Reno. She lit out and never looked back. I heard later that she'd found herself a sugar daddy."

"I'd say you made a great escape."

"That's true enough," he said ruefully. "But I doubt you've ever been deserted like that—it bruises the ego, Nicci."

She couldn't imagine any woman walking away from Trey. Not if she'd really loved him. "Your ego must have healed over time."

"It was a couple of years or more before I met Lacey. She was my age and the single mother of a little two-year-old girl. She worked hard as a waitress, while trying to take college classes on the side. I thought we matched up just fine. And I grew darned attached to the little girl."

"What happened? The baby's father showed up to make trouble?"

He shook his head. "No. He was out of the picture. It was Lacey's family that caused the problems. They were a dysfunctional group, including her parents. Always begging for money or help of some kind. Their interference finally got to be too much."

He was practically describing what Nicole had been going through with her own parents. Had Trey noticed the parallel? Was that why he'd not wanted to take their relationship a step closer to love and marriage?

Trying to quell her runaway thoughts, she asked, "Did you break up with Lacey?"

"No. She packed up and moved her and the baby to California. Ironically, after Lacey left, her family moved away, too. But whether they followed her, I never heard."

"You could've gone after her."

He shrugged. "She obviously didn't care enough to stay with me and try to make it all work, so I didn't see any point of putting up a fight to keep her."

It didn't sound like he'd put up a battle for either woman. In some ways Nicole was glad he hadn't. It could only mean that deep down he hadn't loved enough or cared enough to fight for what he wanted. Only, somewhere along the way, those bad experiences had pushed him into believing he never wanted to be a family man. If that was the case, she might never change his mind.

"I see," she murmured thoughtfully.

A look of disbelief crossed his face. "That's a surprise. I didn't expect you to understand why I'd basically given up on women—until you came along."

She practically stopped breathing as she waited for him to say more. Like how much he would always need her. How much he would fight to keep her in his life. But the silence in the room began to stretch as far as the lingering shadows. And after a while Nicole decided the best and only thing to do for the moment was to show him that she honestly did understand.

Nestling her cheek against the curve of his shoulder, she said, "Before I ever moved here to Arizona, I had promised myself that I wasn't going to look at another man. At least, not anytime soon. Then you walked into Chandler's office and made me break that vow."

His chest shook with a chuckle, and the sound brought a smile to her face. "What's funny about that?" she asked.

"Be honest. I caught your attention because you'd never smelled a man who was covered with cow manure."

She hugged him tighter. "Better than any designer cologne."

His fingertips drew lazy lines upon her cheek as he bent his head and touched the tip of his nose to hers. "And you're better than an armful of paradise," he whispered.

"Mmm," she purred. "Then we'd better not waste the rest of the morning."

"I thought you wanted coffee."

She angled her lips against his. "We'll have plenty of time for that—later."

The waning afternoon was spreading long shadows over Virginia Lasseter's vegetable garden as Nicole followed the woman through rows of snap beans, tomatoes and corn.

Pausing, the tall, slender woman with long dark hair pointed to a portion of the garden to their right. "I normally have cantaloupe and watermelon growing there, but with Harley raising acres and acres of melons, he told me not to bother with those—he'll keep me supplied. So I planted more onions, carrots and radishes instead of melons. Trey hates radishes, but he's rarely around to eat."

Virginia looked at her and smiled, and not for the first time this afternoon, Nicole thought how much Trey's grandmother reminded her of Maureen Hollister. Not that the women's appearances or lives were similar in any way. Maureen was an incredibly wealthy woman and the owner of one of the largest ranches in Arizona. The family's holdings raked in more money in a single year than Nicole could imagine. As for Virginia, she lived in a very modest old house on a small acreage. She worked as a waitress to support herself, and yet she had that same regal quality that Maureen possessed, that same youthful beauty that was timeless. Both women's eyes shone with strength and wisdom. The two important qualities that Nicole often prayed her mother would find.

"I love radishes," Nicole said. "Actually, there's not a vegetable in your garden that I don't like."

"Good. When everything is ready to pick, I'll call you. I'll have plenty to share with you."

"I'd like that."

Virginia's gaze moved from Nicole to where Trey was sitting on the steps of the back porch, playing with one of the woman's several cats.

"I think my grandson disapproves of my decision to marry Harley," she said. "When I showed him my engagement ring, he looked like he'd swallowed a few fence steeples."

Not long after Nicole and Trey had arrived at his grandmother's house, she'd sprung the news of her engagement on them and showed off the hefty sparkler that Harley had slipped onto her finger.

Nicole felt incredibly happy for the woman and had given her a sincere hug and well wishes. As for Trey, he'd mostly remained quiet about the news.

"I wouldn't say he's unhappy, Virgie. I think the word *marriage* just makes him feel a bit squeamish."

The older woman sighed as she tucked a strand of black hair threaded with silver behind one ear. "That's understandable. His parents were always at each other's throats. Our son Amos was, still is, a good man in his own way. But he's the sort that never should've gotten married or been a father. Not that he ever was much of one," she admitted. "When he and Emma divorced, it was a blessing all around. After that, James and I hoped our marriage would be an example for our grandson. But then Trey had some bad tries at romance."

"Yes. He told me a little about them. But I believe he's over that now."

Virginia batted a hand through the air. "Over those women? Pooh. He didn't love either one of those gals in the first place."

Nicole wondered how Virginia could be so certain of her grandson's emotional state. "What makes you think so?"

Smiling, she patted Nicole's shoulder. "I never saw hide nor hair of either one of them. But I've seen you."

Was this woman implying that Trey might possibly love Nicole? Just because he'd brought her here today? No. She'd be foolish to let her hopes go that far.

Nicole was trying to think of some sort of appropriate response when Virginia nudged her shoulder toward the house.

"Let's go in," she said. "I have something to give you."

They strolled back to the porch where Trey still sat with the black cat.

"What are you two doing?" he asked. "I thought you were going to gather the eggs."

"We have plenty of time to do that before dark," Virginia told him. "You just stay put. We have some girl business in the house to take care of."

Trey arched a skeptical brow at his grandmother. "Are you filling Nicci's head with stories about me?"

"I don't want to scare her off," she answered sassily, while gesturing for Nicole to follow her onto the porch.

Trey winked at Nicole. "Okay. You two just go on and leave me all alone. At least, Cleo likes me."

"Cleo likes anybody who'll rub her belly. And by the way, all the cats need their vaccines. Think you can take care of them the next time you come? That's much easier than me hauling seven cats into the clinic."

"I'll bring all the vaccines next time," he promised.

The two women entered the house, and after walking through the small kitchen, Virginia guided her to a small bedroom at the back.

"This used to be Trey's room while he was living with us. That was years ago, before he went to work on the Johnson Ranch. Now I mostly use it to store things," she explained.

The small room had a linoleum floor printed to look like river rock. A single long window covered with sheer priscillas was located next to the side of a full-sized bed made with a wooden bookshelf for a headboard. A matching chest stood across from the bed, and on top of it was a framed photo of Trey that appeared to be taken at his high school graduation. Everything was simple and neat and spotless.

"Trey has confessed he's not much of a housekeeper," Nicole said. "Was his room messy back then?"

Virginia chuckled. "It was usually a disaster. But I didn't clean it up for him. I made him do it."

She moved to the head of the bed where a cedar chest was pushed up against the wall. After removing a small lamp from the top and setting it aside, she pushed up the lid.

Nicole was wondering what the woman could possibly be wanting to give her when Virginia pulled out a handmade quilt.

"I made this many years ago. It's done in a double wedding ring pattern," she said, her hand smoothing over the calico. "For a gift for Trey whenever he got married. I'm giving it to you now."

Nicole's mouth fell open as she handed the quilt over to her. "But Virgie, I can't take this!"

"Why not? I'm giving it to you."

"But Trey is—"

"Trey nothing. He'll come around. Just like I did with Harley," she added with a coy grin.

Nicole was virtually speechless. The mere fact that Virginia Lasseter had accepted her as Trey's girlfriend so quickly and without question was amazing in itself. But to give her such a keepsake was more than she could grasp.

"I don't know what to say, Virgie," she murmured, and then before she could stop them, tears sprang to her eyes. "This is—the most beautiful gift anyone has ever given me."

"Oh, I doubt that. Trey said you were a city girl and wore fancy high heels. I figure you've had lots of nice gifts before."

Was that the way he'd described her? Thought of her? Maybe when they'd first met, she'd seemed materialistic, but surely he'd learned differently now.

Shaking her head, Nicole said, "Virgie, a gift from a store isn't like this one. My home back in Fort Worth—my parents have always had money. But I wish—" She paused and blinked back the moisture burning her eyes. "I wish that home could've been more like yours."

Virginia's understanding smile made it even harder for Nicole to keep from bursting into tears.

"You'll get to do it your way now," she said, curving her arm around Nicole's shoulders and giving them a squeeze.

"But you and Harley will be getting married soon," Nicole reasoned. "You should keep this quilt for the two of you."

"Nonsense. Harley wouldn't care if he was sleeping under a piece of canvas. And you know something, neither would I. We're just going to enjoy each other. In the end that's all that matters."

Blinking back her tears, Nicole planted a kiss on Virginia's smooth cheek. "Thank you. For the quilt. For everything."

"You're welcome. Now come on. Let's go see if Trey's ready for some fried pies and coffee."

The two women started out of the bedroom, only to meet Trey at the open doorway.

"What's the matter?" Virginia asked. "Did Cleo get moody and claw you?"

He glanced at Nicole and then his grandmother. "No. I—uh—was coming after Nicci. I've got to get back to town—to the clinic to meet Doc. As soon as I can get there."

Nicole said, "Chandler never works on Sunday. Has there been an emergency?"

"Not exactly," Trey answered. "Doc needs me for something."

"Well, darn. I wasn't nearly finished visiting with Nicci yet." With a tolerant smile, Virginia patted the middle of her grandson's chest. "You'll just have to bring her back, Trey."

"I will, Granny."

"Soon."

"Yes, soon."

He sounded impatient, which was totally out of character for him, Nicole thought. Even when an emergency arose at work, he always reacted in a cool, efficient manner. But here in front of Virginia was hardly the time to question him. Instead, she said, "I'll go fetch my handbag."

Chapter Eleven

Trey had barely driven away from his grandmother's house when Nicole asked for an explanation.

"I thought you said this wasn't an emergency. Why are you in such a hurry?"

He glanced over to see a confused frown on her face, and for a split second, Trey considered stopping the truck on the side of the road and pulling her into his arms.

From the time he'd made love to her early this morning until now, something had happened to him. Whether it was the way she'd clung to him, or how she'd seemed to understand when he'd talked about his past mistakes, he wasn't sure, but it had felt like some sort of dam had broken inside him. And then when he'd watched the way she and his grandmother had interacted, it was like a foggy lens had been peeled from his eyes.

Before he received Chandler's call, he'd decided that as soon as he and Nicole returned to her place, he was going to have a long talk with her. He was going to put his heart, everything, on the line and find out exactly where he stood with her. She needed to know that he didn't want just an affair with her. He wanted more. Much more. If she wasn't willing to give him those things, he had to be prepared to tell her goodbye.

"It's nothing about rushing to treat a wounded or sick animal," he said. "Doc wants me to go to Phoenix with him—right now. As soon as I get there."

She squared her knees around so that she was looking directly at him. "Phoenix? On a Sunday?"

He grimaced. "I didn't want to say anything in front of Granny. Not that she would've repeated anything to anyone, but it might have worried her. I'll explain everything to her later."

She arched a brow at him. "How about explaining to me now?"

Fixing his gaze on the highway, he said, "The police have set up a meeting with Ginny Patterson. Doc wants me to be there with him."

"Why does Chandler want you with him? He has three brothers who can go."

Her question felt like an ice pick driving right through him. "I guess it's hard for you to understand, but Doc considers me a brother, too."

There was a pause of silence and then she said, "I'm sorry, Trey. I didn't mean it that way. I know that you two are practically tied at the hip. I just thought—well, to be honest, it makes me uneasy to think of you going anywhere near someone who might be a murderer."

"Don't worry. We'll only be listening in on some conversation," he said in an effort to assure her. "And later I think you and me need to talk."

From the corner of his eye, he could see a guarded expression come over her face.

"Talk? About what?"

"Oh, about whether we're going to go panning anytime soon. There's treasure to be found out there, you know."

She reached for his hand, and his heart winced with longing as her fingers tightened around his.

"I do know. And we're going to find it—together."

Trey could only wonder if they were talking about the same kind of treasure.

After dropping off Nicole at her house, Trey drove on to the clinic and found Chandler waiting for him.

"What about your brothers and Gil?" Trey asked as he climbed into Chandler's truck and fastened his seat belt.

"Joe and Connor are already in Phoenix with police detectives. Blake, Holt and Uncle Gil are traveling just ahead of us in another vehicle," Chandler explained. "Normally, we wouldn't be allowed to listen in on something like this, but Gil pulled some strings with the department."

"What about Maureen? Did she go with the others?"

"No. Mom is at home. Being on the ranch gives her comfort."

That was understandable, Trey thought. Three Rivers Ranch had been Maureen's home for more than forty years. "Holt mentioned at the party that this meeting might be happening soon. I wasn't expecting it to be today."

"Joe got a call late last night that things were quickly falling into place." He blew out a long breath and slanted an uneasy glance at Trey. "Guess this is it, buddy. The last chance to find the truth about Dad. If this falls apart, there's nothing else left. It kills me to think of Mom living the rest of her life wondering what really happened to Dad."

"This isn't just about Maureen. It's about you and your brothers, too. You've all suffered over the unknown." Trey glanced at Chandler's stern profile. "Just how much does this Ginny seem to know about your dad's death, anyway? Has she told anyone?"

"She has her suspicions, and that's all that Joe knows. Other than the basic facts that she had some sort of connection to Dad via the Phoenix Livestock Sales and she's scared to death of her husband. Supposedly that's why she's not come forward with information before now. Has to be conscience, or the opportunity to get the husband out of her life, that finally made her agree to help. Take your pick."

"Doesn't matter as long as you find the truth," Trey told him.

Once they arrived at the police department in Phoenix, Trey and Chandler were directed to a section of the building designated for the homicide division. When they entered a small sparsely furnished room used for interrogations, they found Blake sitting at a table, while Gil and Holt were standing together at the back of the room. To one side, three men wearing street clothes were gathered around some sort of technical equipment.

Spotting Chandler and Trey, Gil immediately strode forward and began to explain what was happening.

"Where are Joe and Connor?" Chandler asked, his gaze circling the room. "I thought they'd be here with the detectives. Has the meeting already started somewhere else?"

Gil said, "There's not going to be a meeting. Not in the sense you're thinking. Ginny agreed to having a hidden camera with sound placed in her kitchen. That's the issue that was holding up this whole thing.

To get the bug installed without her husband suspecting or finding out."

Chandler and Trey exchanged looks of surprise.

"You mean this is sort of like a sting?" Trey asked the retired detective.

"Exactly," Gil said. "And frankly in this case, we're at Ginny Patterson's mercy. If she doesn't get her husband to talking, or if she tips him off in any way, this could all be over before it begins."

Chandler groaned. "This is a hell of a situation. She wants us to believe her husband was involved in Dad's death? And not her? How can we trust her on this?"

"We don't have any other choice," Gil said, then motioned for the two men to follow him. "Come on. I'll introduce you to the guys who'll be operating things on this end."

A few minutes later, Holt walked up to Trey and Chandler. A cup of coffee was clutched in one hand, while a frown marred his face.

"This stuff tastes like ground-up parsnips," he muttered as he glanced down at the black liquid. "I wish Jazelle was here to pour me a bourbon and Coke. This waiting around is hell."

"Yeah, it's hell all right," Chandler agreed. "But if you're worried about Maudie foaling tonight, don't be. I checked her before I left. The baby is lying just as he should be."

A half-hearted smile on his face, Holt slapped

a grateful hand on Chandler's shoulder. "Thanks, brother. I'm not worried about Maudie. I just want all of this stuff about Dad to be over and done with. It's been eight, close to nine years since Dad died. It's time for our lives, and Mom's, to move on."

Trey felt the same way. He wanted his relationship with Nicole to move on from what it was now. He wanted to know that she would be with him forever. Not just until she grew bored with him, or decided her family needed her back in Texas. Maybe she wasn't expecting or wanting to hear that he loved her, that his whole outlook about marriage had changed. But one way or the other, she had to understand where his thoughts were headed, and he needed to know whether any of it really mattered to her.

Trey was still deep in thought when one of the technicians suddenly spoke loud enough for everyone to hear. "If you men want to gather round, we're picking up image and sound now."

Trey followed Chandler and his brothers and uncle over to a computer screen on a metal desk.

"I hope to hell the picture gets better than this," Gil said as everyone stared at the grainy images.

The eldest of technicians quickly turned a dial on the machine, and the screen immediately cleared to show an area of kitchen cabinets and one end of a farm table covered with checked oil cloth. The white wooden chairs had lost most of their paint from years of use, but the shabbiness of them or the nearby cabinets was hardly important.

It was the large man sitting at one end that caught Trey's attention. He was a seedy-looking character, somewhere in his late fifties, with thin balding hair combed straight back from a low forehead. His rough features looked puffy, as though he either drank or had some sort of health issue. The dark-colored shirt covering his slumped shoulders looked to be splattered with something like paint or wet concrete. He was forking food into his mouth as fast as he could chew and swallow.

"What is this slop anyway?" the man asked. "I might as well be chewing one of those bones you throw out for the dogs!"

"It's pot roast. I cooked it for you special," a feminine voice spoke from somewhere beyond the table. "You always liked it before."

"Not with these damned rotten teeth!" he bellowed. "I need something soft!"

"I'll fix you some scrambled eggs," she said.

"No, you won't fix me any scrambled eggs," he mimicked, every word dripping with sarcasm. "You'll sit your ass down and quit hovering over me!"

A woman with drooping features and short blond hair pinned out of her eyes came into view as she walked over to a nearby chair and rested her hands on the top of the backrest. She was wearing a cotton housecoat that gaped at her bosom, while the edges of the sleeves were frayed. She hardly looked nervous, Trey thought. Instead, she looked like a person who was merely going through the motions of living.

"You know, Ike, you could get those teeth fixed if I went back to work," she suggested. "I've been thinking I might get my old job at the sale barn again. I hear Walt needs help in the concession now."

The man she called Ike suddenly jerked his head up and stared menacingly at his wife. "You're gettin' damned sassy tonight. You askin' for a beatin'?"

Trey was wondering why the woman was living with this animal of a man when Chandler looked at him and silently mouthed the word *sick*.

On the screen, Ginny moved away from the chair and was out of sight for only a second before she returned with a pitcher filled with tea or some sort of dark liquid. As she refilled Ike's glass, she said, "I'm trying to help. We could use a little more money around here. Especially with you getting fired from that concrete job."

He slapped his fork down so hard that the table actually shook. "That was no fault of mine! And don't you ever mention that sale barn again! You think I'm gonna let you go work there and get yourself another man? You ain't nothin' to look at, but I'll be damned before anybody else gets you!"

To the right of Trey, Holt whispered, "God help her."

On the other side of Chandler, Blake muttered, "I'd like to get my hands around his throat."

Back in the Patterson kitchen, Ginny seemed to gather some energy or courage, or both, as she straightened her shoulders and stared down at her husband. "What are you talking about? Another man? I've never had another man. Why would I want one when I have you?"

Forgetting the food on his plate, Ike glared at her. "Don't stand there and lie to me in that catty voice! I'll knock your head off your shoulders!"

"If you're talking about Joel Hollister, I have a bit of news for you, Ike. I read in the newspaper that the Yavapai sheriff's department has come up with some new evidence that says the rancher wasn't drug to death by a horse—he was murdered. You know anything about that?"

Ike looked like a man who'd just seen the devil and didn't know whether to get ready to fight, or run. But after a moment he quickly gathered himself and sneered at her. "You're worse than stupid. Why would I know anything about that rancher? He was a rich bastard. Somebody killed him for his money."

Seemingly unfazed by his retort, she said, "The law doesn't think so. And I don't think it, either. I believe that you killed Joel Hollister! Just because he was my friend!"

The damning accusations came out of Ginny so suddenly and unexpectedly that everyone in the room stared in stunned fascination at what was unfolding before them.

His voice low and threatening, he said, "I'll give you one thing, Ginny, you got more guts than I ever thought."

Ginny put down the pitcher and moved a few inches on down the table. "Yeah, I finally got enough guts to face the fact that I'm living with a murderer."

An evil grin twisted his face. "Hell yeah, I killed that son of a bitch Joel Hollister. Just what do you think you're going to do about it?" he goaded. "I'll tell you what. Not one damned thing. Or I'll smash your head the same way I did his!"

"That's it," Blake said in a hushed, incredulous voice. "We got him!"

While Holt was making a fist pump, Trey was expecting the woman to run out of the house and to safety. Instead, she continued to stare at him as though she wanted to go after him with a carving knife.

"Why, Ike? You never knew the man. He didn't do anything to you."

"Nothin'? He was going to help you leave me. Yeah, I knew about the plans you two made. You think I'm as dumb as you are, but I'm not. Back then, you were actin' awful happy for some reason. I couldn't figure out why until I heard you on the phone talkin' to Wanda, that loopy old friend of yours. Hollister was gonna help you get you and your things to the bus station without me knowin'."

Ginny blinked, and Trey prayed she wouldn't break down now.

"No one else around here ever had the guts to help me—except for Joel," she said. "I'll never forgive myself for asking him—for causing his death."

"Aw now, ain't that sweet," he drawled sarcastically. "You think the man died a hero."

Trey noticed Ginny's hand wrap around the handle of the heavy glass. Was she going to use it as a weapon? Why didn't she just get the heck out of there?

Trey was about to whisper the question to Chandler when he saw Ike pick up his fork and point it at Ginny in a bullying manner.

"In case you'd like to know, I didn't find out the man was a rich, well-to-do rancher until the next day. That's when I called Hollister and told him I wanted to meet him. I made up this cock-'n-bull sob story about how much I loved you and wanted him to help me win you back. Just like I figured, he didn't want his family knowin' he was mixed up with a woman like you, so he agreed to meet me on the backside of the ranch."

"That's where you killed him," she stated in a stricken voice.

"It was so easy it was pitiful. He turned around to tend to his horse and never knew what hit him. At first, I didn't plan on making it look like an accident. That came to me after the fact. Worked, too, didn't it? Joel Hollister was drug to death by his own trusty steed. That's what the newspapers all printed." His laughter was a satanical sound. "You know, Ginny, the only thing I regret is that I didn't get some money out of him before I killed him. That was stupid of me, but a man can't think of everything."

"No. You never thought of the most important thing," Ginny dared to say.

"What's that?"

"Good lawmen don't give up on righting an evil wrong. And you're evil, Ike. Right down to the core."

"Somebody needs to get her out of there! The monster will kill her!" Blake moved desperately toward the screen as if he could pluck Ginny out of danger.

"Hang on, Mr. Hollister," one of the detectives assured him. "Officers will be moving in any second."

Trey was about to echo Blake's fears when Ginny suddenly threw the glass pitcher directly at Ike's face.

Roaring and sputtering, he jumped to his feet, but by then three detectives burst into the kitchen and quickly shackled his hands behind his back.

When the video feed went dark, Ike was cursing a blue streak and Ginny was weeping.

The room full of men went quiet until Gil finally turned to face his nephews. His usual swarthy complexion had gone pale and his features were taut. No doubt he'd been struck hard by what they'd all just witnessed.

After clearing his throat and wiping a hand over his face, he said, "I don't know about you guys, but that was damned hard to watch—to hear why my brother died."

Blake stepped forward and placed a hand on his uncle's shoulder. "Hard, but necessary. Everything is going to be good now, Gil. Especially for Mom. And that's what matters the most."

Gil gave his eldest nephew a grateful nod. "Yes, she does matter the most. And if any of you are wondering about the legal end of this, I'm fairly certain the DA of Yavapai County will prosecute Ike Patterson. A lawyer will probably advise him to retract his confession, and there might be a fight about entrapment, but one way or the other, he'll pay for his crime."

Beside him, Trey could hear Chandler let out a long breath of relief. A reaction, not only to the end result of tonight, but to years of unanswered questions.

Holt said, "I don't know how the rest of you feel, but I think Ginny Patterson deserves a medal for bravery."

"I damned well second that," Chandler added. "He would've killed her. Maybe not tonight, but at some point in the coming days, he would've silenced her."

"Poor, poor woman," Trey said. "All these years

with no one to help. Except for your dad. And he died trying."

Chandler looked at him, and Trey didn't miss the mist of tears in his friend's eyes.

His voice raw, Chandler said, "Dad died because he loved helping people. He wanted everyone to be as happy as he was."

Gil said, "You're right, Chandler. And that's the way we're going to honor Joel. Let's go home and be happy."

As Trey followed the Hollister men out of the interrogation room, he couldn't think of anything he wanted more.

Monday mornings were always chaotic at the clinic, but that didn't stop the staff from celebrating the happy news that Joel's murderer had been arrested and would likely remain behind bars.

Knowing the Hollisters had suffered for years over the ordeal, Nicole was thrilled for all of them. The family could finally put the how and why of that awful incident to rest. But at the moment, Nicole wasn't celebrating; she was doing her best to stop a flow of tears from streaming down her face.

Why, oh why, had she answered her cell phone? One glance at the ID had told her the call was from Texas. She should've ignored it. But the waiting room had momentarily cleared and the business phone was quiet. And since her father often updated his cell phone, she'd feared it might have been him calling to tell her that Angela had relapsed with another mental breakdown. Instead, she'd been totally shocked to hear Randy Dryer's voice in her ear.

The Hollisters weren't the only ones who could put the lid on an unpleasant memory, she thought, as she dabbed a tissue to the corners of her eyes. And now that she had a moment to think, she realized she was thankful for the call. For so many reasons, it had been cathartic.

"Wow! No one in the waiting room and the phone is quiet! Ready for some lunch?"

The sound of Trey's voice entering the room had Nicci sniffing back her tears and swiveling her chair to face him.

"Hi, Trey! Uh—yes—I'm ready for lunch." Another pesky tear slipped from the corner of her eye, but she managed to give him a bright smile. "I'm—"

As soon as he spotted the tears on her cheeks, his smile turned into a frown. "Are you crying? What's wrong? This is a happy day! You're supposed to be celebrating."

Gripping the tissue, just in case she might need it again, she rose from the chair. "I know I'm supposed to be happy. And I am, really. I just need a moment to compose myself."

He frowned as he eyed the cell phone lying on the desk. "Why? Has your mother been giving you a bad time? Is that it?"

"No. I—" She paused as she tried to think of the right way to explain her emotional state without sounding crazy. "Mother hasn't called yet today, thank God. But I did get a call from Texas—from my old boyfriend—Randy Dryer."

One of his brows cocked to a skeptical arch. "The man who asked you to marry him?"

Nicole's stomach roiled at the very thought. There would never be any other man in the world for her except Trey.

She took a step toward him, and in a hurried voice answered, "Yes. The one I turned down. He—uh—he's a marine now and back in Fort Worth for two weeks and wants me to fly back and join him. He's dropped his current girlfriend because he says he still wants to marry me."

One of the things she'd always adored about Trey was that he had such an expressive face. His eyes and mouth, even the dimples in his cheeks, were constantly revealing his thoughts and feelings. But now as she looked at him, all she could see was a stone-faced stranger.

"Oh, I see."

The odd expression on his face and the three-worded response were hardly what she'd expected from him.

Frowning with frustration, she said in a wary tone, "I'm not sure that you do."

"Don't worry, Nicci. I get the whole picture—

now. Those are happy tears. Congratulations. I can't say that I blame you for changing your mind. I hear that's a woman's privilege, and God knows I've learned that the hard way. How soon will you be going back to Fort Worth? Does Doc know yet that he's going to have to find a new receptionist?"

She was so stunned by his questions that her whole body began to quiver. But the reaction was only momentary as, right behind the shock, anger poured through her, causing her cheeks to redden and her hands to clench into fists. How dare he assume something so ridiculous! The man had shared her bed. Did he not know her at all?

She forced her gritted teeth to relax enough to push a retort past her lips. "I haven't decided yet! It might be sooner than you think!"

Before he could make a reply, a buzzer announced the door of the main entrance being opened, and Nicole looked across the waiting area to see a beagle trotting into the room followed by a young woman holding the dog's leash.

Oh great, this was a fine time for an interruption. She turned back to Trey to tell him she'd talk with him later, but there was nothing but empty air in front of her.

He'd walked off without a word. He was accepting without a fight what he thought was her decision to marry Randy. Apparently, he was going to let her go just as he'd let the other women in his past walk away. So much for hoping he might actually love her, she thought sadly.

Drawing in a deep, bracing breath, she blinked her eyes and walked over to the woman standing at the check-in counter.

Any other time, Trey would've been thrilled that he and Chandler were headed to the Johnson Ranch. Trey would always be a close friend to Mr. Johnson, the man who'd single-handedly persuaded Trey to enter the profession of animal welfare. Along with seeing Mr. Johnson again, Chandler was in an especially jovial mood. From the moment he'd arrived at the clinic this morning, the veterinarian had been laughing and joking. Trey wanted to join in on the man's merriment, but how could he feel any sort of happiness when his heart felt like two hands had torn it right down the middle?

He was deep in the misery of his thoughts when Chandler's hand suddenly landed with a loud pop on the console between their seats.

With a visible jerk, Trey whipped his head around. "What the hell was that for?"

"I'm trying to wake you up! I've been talking to you for the last five minutes and getting no response. Haven't you heard anything I've said?"

Trey's shoulders slunk as he fell back against the truck seat. "No. Sorry. I've been thinking."

"Is that what you call it? I'd call it sulking."

Frowning, Trey cut his eyes toward Chandler. "Okay, I'm sulking. Who gives a damn anyway? I hope we get this job over early. I'm going to the Fandango tonight and getting drunk! I don't care how long it takes me. Or if Joe hauls me off to jail for public intoxication."

Chandler shot him an indulgent look. "I don't have to remind you that intoxication is a fool's remedy. What's brought on this sour mood? You were fine until lunch."

"Something left a bad taste in my mouth. Mainly a strawberry blonde who has a horrible penchant for talking on the phone."

Chandler's laugh was loud and long. "Hell, Trey. She's a receptionist. It's her job to talk on the phone."

"This has nothing to do with her job," he argued. "Did you know that she's constantly getting calls from her mother? That sometimes she even turns off the phone so she won't hear it?"

Chandler shrugged. "I'm aware that her mother is problematic. But I'm sure all of that is going to get better. Once Mrs. Nelson accepts the fact that Nicci isn't going back to Texas."

Trey's teeth snapped together. "That's where you're wrong," he muttered, then shook his head. "I shouldn't be the one to tell you this, Doc, but Nicci *is* going back to Texas. She's going to marry that marine she used to date."

Chandler laughed again. "You're messed up, Trey.

I think you need to take off tomorrow and get some rest."

"Right. I'll need it to nurse my hangover," he agreed in a petulant voice. "Guess this will teach you not to be hiring city girls. I tried to tell you she wouldn't last. The only thing that surprises me is that she hung around for this long!"

Losing his patience now, Chandler pulled the truck to the side of the highway and braked the vehicle to a jarring halt. "Gabe is waiting on us right now! But I'll be damned if we go to the Johnson Ranch before you explain all of this to me. And not in those damned innuendos!"

Lifting his hat from his head, Trey raked both hands through his hair as he related the whole encounter he'd had with Nicole and then ended it with a self-directed curse word. "I was a fool, Chandler. That's all. I should've never let myself get to thinking that she could seriously care for me."

"She does seriously care for you. Are you an idiot?"

Trey leaned his head toward the passenger window and stared at himself in the side mirror. "Yep. That's me."

Chandler muttered a curse. "Tell me this, Trey. What did Nicci say when you left her desk?"

"Nothing. She went to wait on Mary Ferguson and her beagle. I didn't hang around to hear more. And what else could I say?"

"Damned plenty!" Chandler blasted at him. "Why didn't you grab her up and tell her you loved her? Why didn't you say there was no way in hell you'd ever let another man have her? That he'd have to go over your dead body to get her!"

Trey's mouth fell open as the gist of Chandler's words slowly sank in on him. "I've messed up."

Chandler made an impatient sound. "Did she say that she loved this guy? Did she come right out and say she wanted to marry him?"

"No. Not that I can remember, but as soon as she said the word *boyfriend*, my brain turned to scrambled eggs. Besides, she was crying. And she said she was happy. And that's the way I want her to be."

"Yeah, you've messed up." He put the truck in gear and gunned the vehicle back onto the highway. "But I wouldn't worry. Nicci will forgive you for being a lamebrain."

She might forgive him for being stupid, Trey thought miserably. But what about the rest? Like loving him. Marrying him.

"I'll talk to her tonight."

"If I was you, ole buddy, I'd be doing more than talking. You might think about stopping by the flower shop before you see her."

Chandler reached for the knob on the radio and tuned it to Trey's favorite station. As soon as the Frank Sinatra tune floated out of the speaker, Trey turned a grateful look on him.

"Thanks, Doc."

"Brothers have to help each other out at times. That's the way I see it."

That's the way Trey saw it, too.

"Nicci, what were you thinking?!" Roslyn exclaimed as she scrubbed a wire dog crate with disinfectant. "Why didn't you run after Trey and explain exactly what was going on with you? Now the poor guy thinks you're going back to Texas to marry Randy!"

At thirty minutes past closing time, the front door of the clinic was locked and Nicole had gone back to the recovery room to help Roslyn with the last of the cleaning chores.

"I was about to explain everything to him when Mary Ferguson walked in with her beagle." Nicole sprayed cleanser on a countertop and methodically wiped the hard surface, while wishing she could wipe that whole scene with Trey out of her mind. Yes, she'd handled the whole thing badly, but he hadn't exactly been a model of common sense.

"Oh pooh! Mary wouldn't have cared if you'd made her wait!" Roslyn straightened up from the cage and leveled a pointed look at Nicole. "I think you were too afraid to tell Trey that you love him. That's what this is all about."

Clutching the disposable cloth in one hand, she walked over to where Roslyn was standing. "That's not so!" she exclaimed, then followed it with a miserable groan. "I—well, it was hardly the perfect time or place."

Roslyn rolled her eyes toward the ceiling, while across the room a dog barked in protest.

"Perfection doesn't fix things. Honesty does," Roslyn said. "Does Trey know you've fallen in love with him?"

"I'm not sure if he's guessed how I feel about him," Nicole said. "But I've showed him in plenty of ways that I love him."

Roslyn shook her head. "But have you said the words to him? Have you made it clear that you're totally besotted with him?"

Clasping her hands behind her back, Nicole walked over to the rows of stacked crates where a few dogs were recuperating until they were well enough to go home. As soon as the dachshund noticed that Nicole was headed in his direction, the bark turned into a happy whine and his tail started wagging.

"Not exactly. I've thought about it, but—I felt like it was a bit soon to spring that on him. And—well, to be honest, I have been afraid. Trey hasn't said anything to me about his feelings or the future." She poked a finger between the wires and stroked the dog's nose. His tail thumped harder. "He told me about those women who left him and how it felt to be deserted. Now I guess he thinks I'm deserting him, too. Oh, Ros, I don't know what to do."

Roslyn turned the crate upside down to drain before she walked over to Nicole. "He and Chandler should be home from the Johnson by dark. You need to be at Trey's place—waiting for him. That way he can't run. He'll have to hear you out."

Nicole frowned. "Why couldn't he run off? If he drives up and sees my car, what's to stop him from turning around and leaving?"

"You think he's that angry with you?"

Angry? The more Nicole pondered it, the more she'd decided the look on his face had been bottom-of-the-pit disappointment. That was even worse than anger.

"No. But he—"

"No buts!" Roslyn interrupted. "This isn't a time to pussyfoot around. You need to be lying for an ambush."

Nicole laughed in spite of her misery. "You've been watching too many Westerns."

"I don't need to watch a Western to know how to deal with a man. But it helps," Roslyn said with a chuckle.

Nicole's mind had already moved on to planning mode when Cybil stuck her head around the door.

"Hey, you two, I'm going home. Are you going to lock up?"

"I'll take care of it," Roslyn answered her. "See you tomorrow."

After the blonde disappeared from the doorway, Roslyn turned back to Nicole and smiled.

"Go home and change, then get over to Trey's house. And don't worry. When he gets home, you'll know what to do."

Trey wasn't coming home. Not anytime soon, Nicole decided. Roslyn had predicted the two men would be home by dark, but twilight had come and gone and now the only light that remained was coming from the yard lamp.

From her seat in one of the wooden rockers, she gazed down the dirt lane that led to Trey's house and desperately wished his headlights would appear. Was she crazy for sitting here in the dark, waiting for a man who probably wouldn't want to see her, much less talk to her?

She loved him more than anything. She'd sit here all night if it would help right things between them. No, she'd camp here on his porch for days, even weeks, if that's what it took to convince Trey that the life she'd led in Texas was truly behind her.

The sound of her ringing phone jerked her from her swirling thoughts, and she hurriedly fished it from the handbag sitting next to her feet.

"Nicci, where are you?"

Nicole frowned at Roslyn's abrupt question. "Silly, where do you think I am? I'm sitting on Trey's front porch—waiting. He's still not here! I'm beginning to think he's probably gone to the Fandango or somewhere to have a few beers."

There was a short silence and then Roslyn said, "He's not doing anything like that. I just got a call from Chandler. There was some sort of accident on the Johnson Ranch. Something about Trey having a run-in with a bull. The men are on their way to the hospital in Wickenburg."

Her heart was suddenly pounding. "Hospital! What's wrong? Is it serious?"

"Sorry, I don't know. Chandler didn't explain. He promised to call me later—after Trey is examined."

Nicole shouldered her handbag as she hurried off the porch. "I'm on my way!"

"Go ahead and kick my rear, Doc," Trey said. "If I'd had my mind on my business, none of this would've happened."

"Forget it. We'd already finished the job," Chandler told him as he walked alongside the wheelchair being pushed by a male nurse. "And you'll mend all right. You just remember what I told you earlier."

Trey looked ruefully down at the cast on his left forearm. He was going to be hampered by the cracked bone for a month, but he could deal with the nuisance. All that mattered to him now was convincing Nicole that the only man she belonged with was him.

"About Nicci, you mean?"

"Exactly," Chandler answered. "It's only nine thirty. You still have time to go by her house."

"Can't. I penned the horses for work tomorrow," Trey told him. "They'll need to be fed and watered."

"Forget about the horses. I'll go by your place and take care of them. Besides, you've been administered pain meds. You don't need to be stumbling around in the dark, trying to carry a heavy feed bucket."

"You shouldn't be trying to feed livestock tonight," the nurse said. "You need to go straight to bed."

Trey couldn't argue with that advice. The only thing that could cure him was to go to bed with a strawberry blonde with a pair of soft lips and more love in her heart than he had a right to. But would she be willing to look past the blockheaded way he'd behaved this morning?

The three men passed through a glass door and onto a concrete area covered by a large overhang.

"I'll go get the truck and pick you up here at the curb," Chandler told him. "No need for you to walk."

"Heck! I'm getting out of this thing!" Before the nurse could stop him, Trey jumped out of the wheelchair.

Seeing it would be useless to argue, the nurse handed him several sheets of paper stapled together. "Here are the instructions to follow. And don't forget to make an appointment with your regular caregiver."

"Don't worry, he will," Chandler said. "And I see her coming right now."

Her? Dear God, he'd finally gone and done it, Trey thought. He'd driven Chandler crazy.

Glancing around, he saw Chandler grinning at the woman trotting toward them.

Nicole!

Stunned, Trey watched her rapid approach. Roslyn must have told her about the accident, he decided. But why had she bothered to come?

Standing next to him, Chandler said, "You don't need me any more tonight, buddy. You're going to be in good hands."

Chandler walked off in the direction of his truck at the same time Nicole rushed up to Trey. Her face was white, and for a split second he thought she was going to burst into tears. Had she actually been that concerned about him?

"Will this young woman be taking you home?"

Compared to the doubts swirling in Trey's mind, the nurse's question was trivial.

"Yes. I'll be taking him home," Nicole answered. She leveled a pointed look at Trey. "And I'll be taking care of him."

"Then you're all set to go, Mr. Lasseter." After winking at Nicole, the nurse said to Trey, "And don't be running into any more bulls. We don't want to see you back here at the hospital."

Trey thanked the nurse, and once the man departed with the wheelchair, he turned to Nicole and said, "You really don't have to do this, you know."

"Do what?" she asked.

In spite of the medication they'd given Trey to dull the pain in his arm, Trey's heart jumped into a runaway rhythm.

"Give me a ride—or anything." He grimaced as he realized he didn't make any more sense now than he had this morning. "I mean, uh, not unless you want to."

Her lips pressed together. "Do you feel like walking out to my car? If your legs are wobbly, I can pull up here to the curb."

"I can walk. Let's go."

Both of them remained silent as they made their way to her vehicle, but as soon as they were seated inside, she turned to him.

"What's wrong with your arm? What happened?"

"It's just a crack. I'll be fine in a few weeks," he said. "I wasn't paying attention, and about the time I stuck my arm through the slats of a loading chute, a bull shot forward and tried to wrap it around an iron pipe."

"Oh." She released a long breath with the one word. "I'm glad you weren't hurt worse."

He gestured toward the keys dangling from her hand. "Aren't you going to start the engine?"

"Not yet. There's something I want to say first. About this morning and the—"

"Just tell me one thing, Nicci," he swiftly interrupted. "Are you going back to Texas and marrying that marine?"

She looked thoroughly disgusted. "You still have to ask those questions? I feel like cracking your skull to match your arm! I'd never marry Randy. Not in a million years. Nor will I be moving back to Texas for any reason. If you hadn't been so quick to assume the worst this morning, I could've explained. But you made me angry. And then you made me even angrier when you left without—" She paused and shook her head. "As though you didn't care at all!"

Groaning, Trey used his good arm to reach for her shoulder and drag her toward him. Once her face was nestled against his neck, he said against the top of her head, "I realize I was wrong. I should've howled in protest. I should've told you that you're my woman— the woman I love—and that I'll never let you go."

She tilted her head back far enough to look at him, and as Trey studied the doubtful shadows in her eyes, he realized she'd been just as uncertain about his feelings as he'd been about hers.

"You love me?" she asked. "Honestly?"

"Honestly. I should've told you that days ago," he admitted. "But I thought it was impossible for a woman like you to love a man like me. I was afraid to risk my heart. Afraid you'd end up leaving me."

"I love everything about you, Trey. Everything! And you might as well get ready to put up with me for the rest of your life, because I'm not going to let you go. Not for any reason!"

His hand cradling the back of her head, he eased his mouth down on hers and kissed her with all the love and tenderness his heart had to give.

When the kiss finally ended, he whispered against her lips, "Let's go home. Like the nurse said, I need to be in bed."

She let out a sexy chuckle. "What about your arm?"

He rested his cheek against hers and wondered if he could possibly be any happier than he was at this very moment. "I'm feeling no pain."

Her fingers pushed through the hair above his ear. "That's because the medication has numbed it."

"No. The hurt is gone, my darlin', because I know you love me and you're going to be my wife."

Easing out of his arms, she settled herself behind the steering wheel, and after starting the engine, she cast him a coy smile. "Is that a proposal?"

"Uh, now that you ask, it is," he admitted. "But don't worry, I'll give you a better one tomorrow. With flowers and a ring and—all my love."

"I only need that one thing from you, Trey. And that's your love."

She drove out of the parking lot, and as Trey settled back in his seat, he realized that, like the Hollister men, he was well and truly going home.

Epilogue

Six weeks later, on a hot May night, a large group of friends and family crowded the roofed patio and spilled over into the yard behind Three Rivers Ranch house. Champagne was flowing and spates of laughter drowned out the distant sound of bawling calves being weaned from their mothers. Spring roundup was being planned for next week, but for tonight no one was thinking about riding and branding.

"I've seen some big shindigs here at the ranch," Trey said. "But I believe this is the biggest."

Standing with his arm around the back of Nicole's waist, Trey gazed across the milling throng of people. He'd never seen the Hollisters so jubilant, but he doubted they could be feeling any more joy than he'd been experiencing these past three weeks since he and Nicole had eloped to Reno and spent several days honeymooning in the cool mountains.

Since they'd returned, Nicole had moved all her things into Trey's house and put her property in town on the real estate market. She insisted that the money from the sale of it would eventually be added to their savings for the big ranch Trey had always dreamed about. At first he'd protested about her plans for the money, but she'd managed to convince him that she wanted what he wanted—a perfect place to raise a big family.

Nicole inclined her head to a spot across the patio, where Roslyn and Chandler were speaking with Maureen and Gil.

"That's a whopper of a diamond Gil slipped on Maureen's finger," she remarked. "I can see it flashing all the way over here."

Trey lifted Nicole's left hand and kissed the knuckle just above her wedding ring. "Yours is a fraction of that size, but it means just the same," he told her.

She turned her beautiful smile up at him. "I love my ring. And I love you, too, Mr. Lasseter."

He hugged her closer to his side. "Are you sorry now that you eloped? Instead of staying here and having a fancy ceremony?"

She shot him a quizzical smile. "Are you kidding? And miss all that planning and stress? And my mother smothering me with well-meaning advice? No, thank you. Eloping was the best thing for you and me. It was very romantic with just the two of us."

Neither Trey nor Nicole had known what to expect from her parents when they'd gotten the news that their daughter was married. Fortunately, Big Mike had been full of congratulations, while Angela had seemed to have experienced a wake-up call. Not only had she quit pestering Nicole with whines and demands, but she'd also happily gone with her husband to New Mexico.

"Hopefully your parents are having a second honeymoon right now," Trey voiced his thoughts.

Nicole smiled up at him. "Yes. I think we've been an inspiration for them. And Mom seems like a different person now. I'm actually looking forward to them coming for a visit. Which might be in time for them to attend Maureen and Gil's wedding."

"Doc tells me the ceremony will be held at the church in town," Trey said. "I was surprised. The ranch is such a huge part of their lives. I thought it would take place here."

"I've been told that she and Joel were married here on the ranch, so I'm thinking she probably wants something different with Gil."

From their shady spot in the yard, Trey urged Nicole toward the patio. "Let's go to the bar. I feel a beer coming on."

She laughed. "Beer when there's expensive champagne to be had?"

"I'm a simple guy," he reasoned.

"Okay, simple guy. What else has Doc told you about the wedding?"

"You'll have to ask Ros for more wedding details. That's all I know. But Doc did give me some very surprising news."

"Oh, what's that?"

"The ranch has hired a new man to work with Holt as his assistant trainer. He's supposed to be arriving soon. You know, the family has tried for years to convince Holt that he needed help, but he wouldn't give in. Because he's so damned particular with his horses, Blake says. But now that he's married and helping Isabelle with the Blue Stallion, he's realized he can't keep stretching himself so thin."

"Apparently, Holt must have found a guy he can trust to do the job the way he wants it. The way Chandler trust you," she added proudly. "The longer I work at the clinic, the more I realize why he wants you to study for a veterinary degree. He needs you in that capacity. But of course, that's a choice you'll have to make."

Trey had been giving the idea more and more thought. But now that he and Nicole were married, there were other things to consider. Not for anything did he want to put a hardship on her, and yet he knew that if he did decide to enter veterinary school, she would give him her total support and never complain. The idea that she loved him that much made him realize just what a blessing he'd been given.

"Hey, you two! Over here!"

They both paused, then seeing Chandler standing at the far end of the portable bar sipping from a fluted glass, they grabbed their drinks and walked over to join him.

"Quite a party, isn't it? Mom is walking on a cloud."

"She looks like a dream, too," Nicole added. "You must be so happy for her."

"And there's something else we're happy about, too. A few years back, Mom put up a several-thousand-dollar reward for the apprehension of the person or persons who might've had a hand in Dad's death. Joe delivered that reward in person to Ginny Patterson today. She was overwhelmed. The money will help her move to a nicer place. And Joe's halfway convinced the woman to make her home in Wickenburg. He's assured her that no one will ostracize her because of Ike."

"That's great," Trey replied. "All she needed was a little help to turn her life around."

"Speaking of Joe," Nicole said. "Why are he and Connor climbing up on the edge of the fire ring?"

Before Trey or Chandler could speculate, Joseph cupped a hand around his mouth and spoke loud enough for the crowd to hear.

"Attention everyone! As law officials of Yavapai County, Connor and I have the duty of seeing that no one overindulges in spirits tonight. So we're ordering all of you to set your glasses down! No one is allowed another drink for two hours."

Gasps and groans rippled through the crowd.

From somewhere in the crowd, Joseph's father-in-law, Sam, yelled out. "What the hell is this, Joe? Jazelle just poured my bourbon. I'm not going to waste it!"

Joseph and Connor exchanged amused glances before they both burst out laughing.

"Just a little joke, Sam. Connor and I actually want to make an announcement. Everyone is here to celebrate Mom and Gil's engagement. Well, we have something more to add to the merriment. I just learned that Tessa is expecting our third child. And Connor got the news this morning that Jazelle is expecting their second. So drink up everyone. It's a happy night."

As everyone rushed forward to congratulate the two men, Trey felt Nicole's hand wrap around his, and he looked down at the coy smile on her face.

"If we ever expect to have a family as big as the Hollisters', we're going to have to get busy," she told him.

Bending his head, Trey pressed a kiss on his wife's cheek. "I promise we'll get started on that tonight, darlin', as soon as we get home."

* * * * *

For more sweeping Western romances,
try these great stories:

She Dreamed of a Cowboy
By Joanna Sims

Making Room for the Rancher
By Christy Jeffries

Their Night to Remember
By Judy Duarte

Available now wherever Harlequin Special Edition
books and ebooks are sold!

**WE HOPE YOU ENJOYED
THIS BOOK FROM**

**HARLEQUIN
SPECIAL
EDITION**

Believe in love. Overcome obstacles. Find happiness.

Relate to finding comfort and strength in the
support of loved ones and enjoy the journey
no matter what life throws your way.

6 NEW BOOKS AVAILABLE EVERY MONTH!

#2827 RUNAWAY GROOM
The Fortunes of Texas: The Hotel Fortune • by Lynne Marshall

When Mark Mendoza discovers his fiancée cheating on him on their wedding day, he hightails it out of town. Megan Fortune is there to pick up the pieces—and to act as his faux girlfriend when his ex shows up. Mark swears he will never get involved again. Megan doesn't want to be a "rebound" fling. But they find each other irresistible. What's a fake couple to do?

#2828 A NEW FOUNDATION
Bainbridge House • by Rochelle Alers

While restoring a hotel with his adoptive siblings, engineer Taylor Williamson hires architectural historian Sonja Rios-Martin. Neither of them ever thought they'd mix business with pleasure, but when their relationship runs into both of their pasts, they'll have to figure out if this passion is worth fighting for.

#2829 WYOMING MATCHMAKER
Dawson Family Ranch • by Melissa Senate

Divorced real estate agent Danica Dunbar still isn't ready for marriage and motherhood. When she has to care for her infant niece, Ford Dawson, the sexy detective who wants to settle down, is a little too helpful. Will this matchmaker pawn him off on someone else? Or is she about to make a match of her own?

#2830 THE RANCHER'S PROMISE
Match Made in Haven • by Brenda Harlen

Mitchell Gilmore was best man at Lindsay Delgado's wedding, "uncle" to her children and, when Lindsay is tragically widowed, a consoling shoulder. Until one electric kiss changes everything. Now Mitchell is determined to move from lifelong friendship to forever family. It's a risky proposition, but maybe Lindsay will finally make good on her promise.

#2831 THE TROUBLE WITH PICKET FENCES
Lovestruck, Vermont • by Teri Wilson

A pregnant former beauty queen and a veteran fire captain at the end of his rope realize it's never too late to build a family and that life, love and lemonade are sweeter when you let down your guard and open your heart to fate's most unexpected twists and turns.

#2832 THEIR SECOND-CHANCE BABY
The Parent Portal • by Tara Taylor Quinn

Annie Morgan needs her ex-husband's help—specifically, she needs him to sign over his rights to the embryos they had frozen prior to their divorce. But when she ends up pregnant—with twins—it becomes very clear their old feelings never left. Will their previous problems wreck their relationship once again?

HSECNM0321

*Mitchell Gilmore and Lindsay Delgado had been best
friends for as long as they could remember. He was
best man at her wedding, "uncle" to her children
and, when Lindsay is tragically widowed, a consoling
shoulder. Until one electric kiss changes everything.
Now Mitchell is determined to move from lifelong
friendship to forever family—if Lindsay can see that
he's ready to be a family man...*

Read on for a sneak peek at
The Rancher's Promise
*by Brenda Harlen,
the new book in her Match Made in Haven series!*

"Do you want coffee?" Lindsay asked.

"No, thanks."

"So…how was your date?"

Considering that it was over before nine o'clock,
she was surprised when Mitchell said, "Actually, it was
great. It turns out that Karli's not just beautiful but smart
and witty and fun. We had a great dinner and interesting
conversation."

She didn't particularly want to hear all the details, but
she'd been the one to insist they remain firmly within the
friend zone and, as a friend, it was her duty to listen.

"That is great," she said. Lied. "I'm happy for you." Another lie. "But I have to wonder, if she's so great... why are you here?"

"Because she's not you," he said simply. "And I don't want anyone but you."

She might have resisted the words, but the intensity and sincerity of his gaze sent them arrowing straight to her heart. Still, she had to be smart. To think about what was at stake.

"I know you're afraid to risk our friendship, and I understand why. But there's so much more we could have together. So much more we could be to one another. Don't we deserve a chance to find out?"

Before Lindsay could respond to either his confession or his question, he was kissing her.

Don't miss
The Rancher's Promise *by Brenda Harlen,*
available April 2021 wherever
Harlequin Special Edition books and ebooks are sold.

Harlequin.com

HSEEXP0321